THE LAST RIDE

"Let me get out first," the guy with his foot in my face says. He's wearing a black shoe with a pointy toe. A shoe which belongs to a man who knows how to damage a man's ribs with a kick. "Then you get out of the car, Flannery. Keep your eyes in front of you. I don't want you looking at our faces. You understand that?"

He takes his foot off my neck and I manage to uncramp myself and crawl out of the car. I get a look at the one called Connie in the light of the moon, and then somebody comes around from my blind side and slams a punch into my gut.

"Do you get it yet, Flannery?" one of them asks. "We want your nose out of our business and this is the last warning you're gonna get. . . ."

D1239482

SIGNET MYSTERY

The JUNKYARD DOG

ROBERT CAMPBELL

Ø
A SIGNET BOOK

NEW AMERICAN LIBRARY

PUBLISHER'S NOTE

This novel is a work of fiction. Names, characters, places, and incidents either are the product of the author's imagination or are used fictitiously, and any resemblance to actual persons, living or dead, events, or locales is entirely coincidental.

Copyright © 1986 by Robert Campbell

SIGNET, SIGNET CLASSIC, MENTOR, PLUME, MERIDIAN and NAL BOOKS
are published by New American Library,
1633 Broadway, New York, New York 10019

First Printing, July, 1986

1 2 3 4 5 6 7 8 9

PRINTED IN THE UNITED STATES OF AMERICA

1

My name is Flannery. My mother, who died eight years ago of a cancer—may she rest in God's arms—called me James. My father calls me Jim. Friends call me Jimmy. Assholes call me Jimbo.

Let me explain a little something about how I fit into the organization of the Democratic party in the city of Chicago, County of Cook, State of Illinois. I'm not going to tell you everything about it. Who's got a lifetime? That's how long it takes to learn the pecking order, or what the late warlord of the Fourteenth, Eddie Lurgan—God rest his soul—sometimes called the "pecker order."

For fifty years, until his retirement from the fire department, my father, Mike Flannery, was a loyal party worker and a first-class precinct captain. Even though he was Lurgan's right- *and* left-hand man until the old ward leader's death—over there in the Fourteenth on the South Side, where I was born and raised among the Irish—he *still* claims he don't know all the ins and outs.

My father still lives in the Fourteenth. I don't. I live in the Twenty-seventh, west of the Loop, which has Irish, Bohemian, Italian, Polish, German, and some Swedes. Also a good many winos and derelicts, the Twenty-seventh having Skid Row for a gut. We also have our share of silk stockings, businessmen, blacks, and Jewish pawnbrokers.

My old man gave up the big house and moved into a one-room flat after my mother died, and I moved over to the Twenty-seventh because he said I'd never have a chance for alderman in the Fourteenth. Lurgan's only son, George, would inherit. He did . . . one year later, when Lurgan keeled over after eating two plates of corned beef and cabbage at a St. Patrick's Day celebration over to the Sons of Hibernia Lodge.

Delvin, the warlord of the Twenty-seventh and the sewer boss of the city, has no sons. Or daughters, for that matter—a dose of the clap, so they say, having rendered him incapable of same. So the Twenty-seventh, says my old man, is my land of opportunity.

Delvin gives me a job in the sewers. I almost don't take it, but my old man says, "Once you climb out of the shit, you'll never let anybody push you back into it."

I don't work down in the pipes anymore. I'm an inspector, reading meters. Occasionally I look down a manhole to remind myself of my father's good advice.

I'm also a precinct captain for the party. My father says there will come a day when I'll be at least a prince, if not the king. I don't tell him that the world of old pols and patronage is probably doomed. This new mayor promised to dismantle the machine. He ain't got around to it yet. Then, again, maybe he'll decide to do what the last mayor done, and use it if he can. Still and all, it seems to me, the old ways is dying.

I don't really care. I'll enjoy what I got while I can. What my old man don't know is that I've already found my place and my contentment.

There are people who put me in the same bag with the old men who stand in the lobby of public buildings and point out which automatic elevator is empty. They put me on the same shelf with Kippy Kerner, who was given a job in the County Building supervising the man who adjusts the valves on the furnaces, and Billy Swinarski, who sits in front of the city treasurer's office and tells the people who ask that they're in front of the city treasurer's office.

I do a job for the city that really has to be done, and if it don't take me eight hours a day, the time I put in doing what some social workers would be doing makes it a seventy-hour week for me, with sometimes no time off Saturdays and Sundays.

I was going to tell you about the organization, what they call the "machine"—wasn't I?

Well, at the top, you've got the mayor, of course. Also you've got the Democratic party chairman. Once, when Daley ruled, he was both. Like the Russian bosses make themselves the head of government and state.

You've got fifty city wards and thirty suburban wards with a committeeman for each. You've got fifty to seventy precincts per city ward—making about thirty-five hundred precincts—each precinct with a captain and one to six full-time workers, depending on how many jobs the committeeman has in his pocket to hand out. There's thirty thousand jobs. It's called patronage. So one out of ten city workers is a precinct captain.

Next to the mayor, the park district superintendent—who is presently tough Ed Keady, the warlord of the Forty-seventh on the Northwest Side—has the most patronage to give. They give him Parks because he tore the ward out of Republican hands a long time ago. Next comes the president of the county board, who controls an enormous amount of public funds and several thousand patronage jobs.

The sheriff's office is a regular fountain of juice. Among other favors, it supplies badges and guns to big-time contributors and other special persons who like to pack heat and horse around with the law as part-time deputies.

Then comes my Chinaman—who is called a rabbi

in New York, a mentor in the colleges and a political sponsor elsewhere—Delvin, who has plenty of jobs to give out since the shit has to be kept moving.

Now, there's eighty aldermen and committeemen, sometimes known as ward leaders, sometimes known as bosses, sometimes known as warlords. Every alderman ain't necessarily a committeeman, but every alderman has a committeeman behind him.

When I say aldermen and committeemen, I mean women, too. They sometimes wear skirts, but they ask no favors and are likely to kick you in the slats when you ain't looking if you make the mistake of treating them like flowers ... except when they so desire same.

The party does not worry about electing state or national candidates, keeping a working relationship with whoever sits in the White House or the governor's mansion.

The party works to elect the mayor, the aldermen, the committeemen, the county assessor, who is usually Irish, the Democratic county clerk, who is in charge of the election machinery, and the Cook County state's attorney, also Irish. The city clerk is usually Polish. At least one seat on the sanitary district board goes to Greeks. Don't ask me why.

The wards that are worked the best can produce three hundred votes; the best ward, twenty thousand. A captain, like me, asks his people to vote a straight ticket. That means every city employee and his relations by blood or marriage vote straight Democratic. Also anyone who has given me his or her marker for a favor. Also any policemen and firemen living in my precinct, which are not many.

Now you know something about the wheels and gears of the "machine," but you'll agree you don't have a clue about how to run it. Neither do I. I'm just learning.

What I do—besides inspecting the sewers—is pro-

THE JUNKYARD DOG

my family. I admit that I keep the idea in mind that
they'll do me favor for favor when election time
comes around.

What's wrong with that? Helping one another. It's
what friends and families do. I will, however, do
them a favor when asked even if they tell me they're
going to vote Republican or Liberal. I bank on their
integrity when election time comes. I think the people who give me their marker usually pay me back.

I live on the top floor of a six-family tenement on
Polk Street. You got to walk six blocks through Skid
Row, a war zone of abandoned buildings, filthy gut-
ters, wrecked dreams, and trashed lives.

Across the hall at the top of the six flights of stairs
lives a family of seven named Recore, who are nice
people except their youngest, Stanley, likes to pound
on my door in the morning and then run away when
I go to see who it is waking me up. His mother says
it's because he likes me. Maybe he likes me because
I'm one of the few outside his family who understands him when he talks since he's got this trouble
with his speech.

Like last summer he comes into my kitchen when
I'm sitting there having breakfast with a friend and
says, "Jimbly, if you gib me some chawpee and bickets,
I'll gib you some japes." Which means, "Jimmy, if
you give me some coffee and biscuits, I'll give you
some grapes."

His oldest sister is crazy for roller-skating and leaves
the house practically every night wearing a little skirt
that shows the curve of *her* biscuits, and if it wasn't
that she lives so close to home, I would maybe have
taken a nibble when I was without a friend.

Right below me lives Mrs. Warnowski, who lives
alone since her husband, Mooshie, who was a fireman, died just before he was ready to retire out at
full pension. She asks me what I can do for her, and

I'm trying to get her full survivor benefits and maybe
a posthumous citation for her husband, which is
both hard to do since Mooshie don't die in the line
of duty but of drowning when he drives his car off
the road into the lake, knocking down a twenty-
thousand-dollar light standard as he goes.

Across from her lives a nice Jewish couple—Myron
is a teacher and Shirley is a librarian—who have a
little girl that is seven and so smart I think maybe
she'll be the first lady president if somebody don't
get there first.

On the ground floor is Mrs. Foran, who is ninety-
two, and her companion, Miss King, who is maybe
ninety but still does all the work around the flat,
taking care of Mrs. Foran, and doing some baby-
sitting for extra money, too. The word about them is
that Mrs. Foran left her husband sixty years ago to
run away with her lover, Miss King, and they have
been a couple ever since.

There's a Quick-Stop where the downstairs corner
flat would be. A couple of Jewish kids from South
America, Joe and Pearl Pakula, own the place and
support their old mother. They live in two rooms in
the back. I do them favors even though they can't
vote yet, not being citizens. Unlike some precinct
captains I don't vote aliens or the dead. At least not
the long dead.

Joe and Pearl let me use their water faucet on the
side of the store to wash my car. I wash it every clear
Saturday morning.

This Saturday when this all begins, I'm washing
my car like always when Mrs. Klutzman comes down
the street to get something from the grocery store,
and I say, "Hello, Mrs. Klutzman, how's your back?
Did you do like I told you?"

"Mr. Flannery, not only do I do like you tell me,
but already the back is feeling better," she says, put-

ting her hand to her kidney to show me it don't hurt anymore. "It's like a miracle."

"Remember, just a half a caroid tablet, not a whole one, in a little hot water. You should put, maybe, a little lemon, it shouldn't taste like dishes," I tell her. "Where are you off to?"

"I need a milk, maybe a sweet roll for my breakfast before I go to the clinic."

"You're not sick?"

"The Free Abortion Clinic over on Sperry Avenue, you should pardon me."

"Why should I pardon you?" I asks.

"Because maybe you don't approve of what help I try to give these poor foolish children who make a mistake and might otherwise end up with a burden. Being you are a Catholic and all."

"I don't make a case against other people, Mrs. Klutzman. I ain't got enough of my own troubles, and the troubles of my friends, I should go around passing judgment on silly girls who didn't take precautions?"

"Or whatever," she says, fingering her purse and looking troubled.

"*You* got troubles," I says.

"Such a mind reader."

"So, tell me."

She opens the battered embroidered bag she carries and takes out a stained rag wrapped around something. She unfolds it and there's a knife covered in blood laying there. Also I smell ketchup. I stick out a finger and touch the red stuff and smell it. Then I taste it. It's ketchup.

"Is this a joke, Mrs. Klutzman?" I says.

"Look on me. Am I laughing?"

She looks very, very troubled, and not a little frightened.

"This knife was on the step in front of the clinic last night when I leave," she says.

"Why are you carrying it around?"

"I didn't want to scare nobody in the clinic."

"What were you going to do with it?"

"What do I know? Maybe I'm thinking I should find a cop. Maybe not. But when I see you, I know what to do," she says, and hands me the knife. "Also I need a butter, I shouldn't forget."

2

After I wash the car—it usually takes me four hours because I'm doing business all while I'm washing—I walk down to the police station and look up Captain Dominick Pescaro.

"Look at this," I says.

"How long you had that?" he says.

"Four, maybe five hours."

"What you doing carrying around a knife smeared with ketchup?" he says.

"How do you know it ain't blood?" I says.

"If you been carrying it around four, maybe five hours it would be brown."

"See what you can learn when you got friends in high places?" I says.

"Also I got a nose," he says, tapping the side of a honker that you could play like a horn in a parade on St. Anthony's Day. "Where'd you get it?"

"An old lady give it me."

"What are you going to do with it?"

"I'm giving it to you."

"Can you tell me where the old lady got it?"

"It was left in front of the door at the Free Abortion Clinic over to Sperry Avenue."

"That sonofabitch Joe Asbach and his squirrels."

"You know the man who done this?"

"He likes to march around in circles."

"What kind of gentleman is he?"

"The kind who wears a topcoat and a hat on a sunny day."

13

"Is he amenable to reason?"

"He knows his rights and likes to stand on them."

"Mother of God, one of those."

Seven men and three women are marching around when I get to the clinic on Sperry Avenue carrying signs that say, "The Nazis burned the babies at Dachau" and "Murderers, murderers, murderers." I can maybe understand why the women are there protesting the removal of the unborn, but it's a little hard for me to understand what the men are doing there, since they don't have to ever worry about having unwanted visitors in their bellies.

I'm not there to debate, however, but to negotiate, once I come face to face with this Joe Asbach. It's a cool day and those who ain't wearing coats are wearing at least a sweater. A couple of the men is wearing hats. I go up to a woman with red hair and a mole on her chin and I ask her which one, if any, of the men is Joe Asbach.

"The man is a saint," she says.

"All I want is you should point him out to me," I says.

"He should be president."

"You don't have to point the finger, just nod when he passes."

"You're here to do him harm."

"I'm here to join the cause," I says.

I will lie at the drop of a hat if it don't do no individual any harm, prevents hysteria, or cuts through the crap.

"There he is now, getting out of the taxi," she says. "You want I should introduce you?"

"Let me make my own hellos. I'm shy in crowds."

I walk over and take Joe Asbach's elbow. Even though he's over six feet and I'm maybe five feet nine, I walk him about twenty yards away from his people.

"I'm going to assume you mean to take your hand off my arm," he says.

"I moved you away from your people to save you some embarrassment," I says.

"What can you do that would embarrass me?" he says.

"I could step on your shoeshine," I says.

"If that's some sort of street threat, I don't get the meaning," he says.

"You dropped an ugly thing on the doorstep of this lawful establishment."

"Is there an ordinance about losing a knife?"

He doesn't try to cop, so right away I got to think that he's either very dumb or very sure of hisself.

"What would you say if somebody left a knife with red smears all over it in front of your door?" I says.

"I'd say some careless workman left behind a knife with ketchup on it after cutting his sandwich in half."

The smirk on his lips is a beauty. I remembered how my old man used to say, "Which one of us is going to wipe that jam off your kisser?" when I thought I was smarter than him.

"So you're not going to pretend you don't know?" I says. It sounds weak as water even to my ears.

"I'm doing the Lord's work and proud of it," he says with his nose tipping up three inches. "Are you a police officer?"

"I'm not, but see over there? Those are cops in that car."

I don't know if they are cops in the car or not but two guys are sitting in a gray sedan and I figure, what the hell, I got nothing else to threaten him with.

"I've got a permit for this demonstration," he says.

"So what? You're not paying attention. We're back to your shoeshine."

His eyebrows lift. That always gets me. It's a haughty thing to do, and I wish I could do it. But when I lift my eyebrows I just look like I'm about to belch.

"You understand," I says, "I step on your shoeshine —a little guy like me—and you at least got to push me off. I fall to the ground yelling assault. The police rush over to save a respected citizen. I'm a respected citizen. They take you to the slammer. They keep you overnight. It's not too bad, but it's long enough for a gentleman like you to catch body lice . . . or something."

"You're threatening me," he says.

He's got a very curly lip. I wish I could do that, too.

"Mr. Asbach, you're quick. You're very quick. You march all you like, but you don't raise your voice to those people in there. You don't call them filthy names like you done elsewhere. And you don't leave bloody threats on their doorstep."

"Ketchup," he says, as though getting the details straight is very important to us both.

"No more. Please understand," I says. "Otherwise, I'm going to have to come back and step on your shoeshine."

3

My father and me have a meal together every Wednesday night over to Dan Blatna's Sold Out saloon in the Thirty-second over to the Northwest Side in Big Ed Lubelski's ward.

Blatna makes a dish with kielbasa and cabbage that is to die from. Customers come from all over the city and out of town just to make like pigs. I see a sixty-, sixty-five-year-old lady once, wearing an evening dress, a rhinestone tiara, and a chinchilla coat, with her face right down in the dish like she couldn't wait the time it took to lift the fork from the plate to her mouth. She looked up and caught me looking at her, grinned, and went right back to it.

The reason my old man and me go there for our feed is that the old man is loyal to the restaurants and saloons of the Fourteenth and I'm loyal to the restaurants and saloons of the Twenty-seventh. This is the way it's done when precinct captains eat out. You go to your own. You scratch my back and I'll scratch yours.

It's okay to go over to the First for nightlife or a special dinner, but it's good politics to eat in the neighborhood otherwise. But since the old man wants to eat over to his ward and I want to eat in mine, we compromise on Blatna's and the Thirty-second.

While he's having his first boilermaker, he asks me what's new in my precinct. I tell him how I tap Jack Reddy over to Water and get him to turn on the tap

17

for this family that can't pay the bill. I get the gas and electric turned back on for them, too.

"I ask the mother afterwards, are they all right, and she says God bless me because they could maybe do without the lights and heat, but it's hell not being able to flush the toilet when you got six kids and a father-in-law with diarrhea."

"God bless the mothers," my father says. "Is that a favor you owe Jack Reddy?"

"Our books are dead even."

That pleases my father, who likes things to balance, unless you can get the other fellow deeply in your debt.

I tell him about Joe Asbach, the Right-to-Lifers, and the knife.

"Fanatics is a pain," he says. "It's like talking to a rock trying to talk to a fanatic. They stare at you with popped-out eyes no matter what you say, then tell you all over again what they just told you which made no sense. You think you scared him into a state of grace?"

"We'll just have to see. I don't think he scares that easy in the first place, number one. I think maybe some Mick or Polack who loves the Pope . . ."

"Watch what you say about the Holy Father. There could be Protestants in the joint . . ."

". . . and is against what the clinic is doing, makes it easy on this Asbach in the second place, number two. Who cares if there's Protestants in the joint?"

"We don't want strangers overhearing family business. What we say about the Pope is just between us good Catholics."

"I'm not a good Catholic," I says. "I ain't made my Easter duties in fifteen years."

"I ain't made my confession in forty"—my old man grins—"but that's another matter. We know where our hearts is."

My heart and beliefs is out there in never-never

land when it comes to religion, but I don't want to get into that. My old man, like most of his generation, let the women keep the faith, and now that my mother—God rest her soul—is gone, he tells stories of her faithful attendance as if it was him who made the novenas and early Masses.

"Who gives out permits on demonstrations?" I asks.

"Streets and Sanitation. That's Wally Dunleavy's mansion."

"Maybe I'll find out what kind of a permit he gives this Asbach. Maybe he don't give this Asbach a permit with open ends. Maybe Asbach is in violation of code."

"That ain't much of a lever."

I give him the empty hands. When you got nothing, a feather looks like a club.

"By the way," I says to my old man, because he still hangs around different firehouses and knows everything that goes on with firemen, "what do you know about Warnowski, the fireman who drove his car through the rail into the river?"

"He drank like a mackerel."

"Was he loaded when he took the dive in the car?"

"Are you working a favor on his behalf?"

"On behalf of his widow, who is not a well woman and cannot live on half-pension. After all, we're looking at maybe twenty-six days before he goes out with his thirty when he takes his unfortunate dip in the river."

"The man should have floated, alcohol being so much lighter than water and him with his tanks full."

"Be that as it may, he didn't take no persons with him . . ."

"He took a twenty-thousand-dollar light pole . . ."

". . . and there's a person who says he swerved to avoid killing a cat."

"The person who says that is another fireman who claims he just happened to be walking along that stretch of road when Warnowski got wet," my old man says, winking at me.

While we're talking about this and that like this, the old man drinking boilermakers and me drinking seltzer water, and both shoveling in the sausage and slaw, Dan Blatna comes over to say hello and to tell me a fellow named Pakula wants me on the phone.

"Who is Pakula and what kind of name is that?" my old man asks.

I tell him it's Jewish South American and it's the grocery boy who has the store downstairs from me.

"Don't let him sell you anything ain't kosher," my old man says, making for him what is a joke, and I go to find out from Joe Pakula that some sonofabitch has touched off a bomb over to that abortion clinic on Sperry Avenue and my good friend, old lady Klutzman, is in the hospital.

4

We get over to Sperry Avenue. There is firemen playing hoses on the storefront clinic, which has it's plateglass window blown out and the side door hanging on its hinges. An ambulance is taking off around the corner and another one is standing by should they find somebody else in the ruins.

There is three loads of uniforms and two detectives, all of which I know. They say "Hello, Mike" to my old man before they say "Hello, Jimmy" to me. That shows respect for the older generation.

I go up and say "Hello, Francis" to Francis O'Shea and "Hello, Murray" to his partner, Murray Rourke.

"Is this arson, a gas explosion, or a bombing?" I says.

"This is none of your business," O'Shea says.

He's a big man with a face like a raw side of beef which has got a kidney for a nose. The busted blood vessels in the nose and across his cheeks looks like a precinct map of the city. I never see him when he ain't on the prod. Maybe this is because he's almost always the man sent out to pick up pieces too ugly for other people to pick up. Other precincts call him in to do their dirty work. He is also type-cast as the bad cop for interrogations.

"A friend of mine was hurt in there," I says.

"There's one dead, a young girl maybe sixteen . . ."

"That's not my friend. My friend is an older lady."

"Mrs. Klutzman," Rourke says. "They took her to Passavant, which has got a trauma center."

He's O'Shea's opposite; slender, clean-cut and clean-shaven, with a complexion like a choir boy's. I see him question a multiple killer so sweetly that the perpetrator is crying over memories of his mother and Thanksgiving dinner. I also see him stomp a fool which has got fifty pounds on him into a sewer grate.

"So, that's two," my old man says. "Any more?"

"Well, that depends on how you look at it," says O'Shea, whose six brothers and sisters is priests and nuns. "The girl was carrying."

"Can we go inside?" I says.

"Watch you don't fall through the hole in the floor, Flannery. We shouldn't want you should break a leg," O'Shea says.

"Are you mad at me, Francis?" I says.

"Just the world."

"Well, all right. That I can understand."

Inside it's a mess. Plastic-covered chairs are smoldering and making a plastic stink. There is glass everywhere. Through the door, in the room where they do what they do, is a hole in the floor. A table with chrome-plated stirrups is tipped over the edge like somebody drove it into a ditch. There's blood all over the place. It ain't been so long since it happened, but it's already turning brown, so I find out that Pescaro is exactly right in what he tells me about the appearance of old blood.

Forensics is already on the scene. I recognize Spidone from the bomb squad. He's picking up pieces of metal with tweezers. I don't have to ask about arson or gas explosions anymore.

A woman in a white jacket and suede knee-length boots over tight jeans is standing there with her hands over her face, looking through her fingers like a child playing peekaboo. I think maybe she's about to be hysterical. I take her wrists in my hands.

We're the same height almost and we're looking at each other eye to eye.

"Are you all right," I says.

"I think I'm going to scream," she says. "No matter where I look, there's pain. No matter how I try to help, there's death."

"Maybe you should get out of this room. If you go sit in what was the waiting room, I'll be out in a minute and take you home in my car."

"I got to go to the hospital."

"Where are you hurt?"

"You don't understand. I'm a nurse at Passavant and I have the next shift."

"I'm going there, too. So, we'll go together. Just give me a minute."

She looks at me for what seems like a long time, like she wants to see, Can she trust me for a ten-block drive. Then she nods and goes out to the waiting area.

I go back to Rourke and O'Shea.

"Is there anybody can tell me anything?" I asks O'Shea.

"Jimmy," he says, "this is a police matter, can't you see? We ain't slow."

"The old lady is a friend. Let me satisfy myself."

"We already asked the questions," O'Shea snaps at me.

"For Christ's sake, O'Shea," Rourke says, telling him to ease up.

"All right. Question whoever you damned well please. You're already making time with one witness. That shine over there is the other," O'Shea says.

"You shouldn't use words like that, Francis, it ain't right," I says.

I go over to talk to the young black man wearing what they call granny glasses. Behind the little round lenses his eyes look like smashed olives, all blurry with pain.

"You all right?" I says.

"I'm not wounded, if that's what you mean," he says.

His eyes flick over to O'Shea, and he makes a face like his stomach just turned on him.

"Oh," I says, "don't let O'Shea bother you. Was you going to step in front of a truck, Francis would be the first man would throw himself at you to try to save your life."

"Ah, then it's *Saint* Francis, is it?"

"Did you say something clever?"

"Saint Francis and the animals?"

"You don't have to explain. I know my calendar of saints."

"Then you get my meaning?"

"Sure, and I hope you get mine," I says. "We all got our reasons for what we think we like and don't like. A man tries to save my life, I don't care he don't want me to marry his sister."

"You're another sonofabitch, aren't you?"

"No. I just decided some time ago not to change the world. I do the best I can do . . . like Francis."

He shrugs his shoulders, and all the starch goes out of him.

"What the hell," he says, "so do I."

"You a volunteer here?"

He nods.

"You an orderly here?"

He blows through his nose like he's disgusted with me, but what can you expect from an Irish bigot. "I'm the doctor here. At least tonight I was the doctor here."

"You perform the abortions?"

"The women don't seem to mind if they want the procedure badly enough."

"That's not what I meant. How many you do tonight?"

"Three. The dead girl was going to be the fourth."

"You already examined her?"

"Yes."

"Where was you when the bomb went off?"

"In the office. I always leave the examining room while Mary Ellen Dunne explains to the patient about the procedure and what she's expected to do after."

"Mary Ellen Dunne's the nurse with the suede boots?"

"She works at Passavant . . ."

"She told me . . ."

". . . and works free shifts here just like I do."

"Why do you leave the examining room while Mary Ellen Dunne explains the procedure?"

"Women need other women at times like the ones that bring them here. I don't want them to feel as though they're nothing but cattle just passing through under the curette. I don't want their personhood taken away from them."

"After Mary Ellen Dunne's told them what's what, do you come back to do the operation?"

"No, there's a small operating room down the hall. The aide—Mrs. Klutzman was our aide . . ."

"She's the main reason why I'm here . . ."

". . . gets it ready while Mary Ellen Dunne talks to the patient. When she's done, she takes the patient into the operating room, where the patient undresses from the waist down and gets into the stirrups under a sterile sheet."

"So you were in your office when the bomb blew?"

"That's where I was."

"Just ready to go in and do the procedure?"

"Waiting for the knock on the door."

"You have any enemies?" I says.

His eyes flick over to O'Shea, who's on the eary. "You mean any personal enemies?"

"That's what I mean."

"No. But when you're my color in Chicago, you never know."

"You have to go through the waiting room to get to the office?"

"No, but I have to pass the doorway to it."

"How many people were out in the waiting room?"

"I don't know. I think I remember three. Another girl with an old woman, and a man."

"Sitting together?"

"I don't know if they were together. If I remember right, the girl and the old woman were sitting down, and the man was just walking in. I don't know if he sat down next to them."

"Old man? Young man?"

"Oh, I see. It wasn't the grandfather. I don't think it was the girl's boyfriend, either. A skinny white man, youngish, but losing his hair."

"Thank you for your cooperation," I says.

"Hey!"

I stop at the doorway.

"You didn't ask my name or shake my hand," he says, very sarcastic.

"I'm sorry," I says. "It wasn't on purpose. I got a head full of troubles and a worried heart."

5

I ask O'Shea and Rourke, who is standing with my old man, where the girl and the old man are and where the skinny white man is.

"Long gone by the time we got here," Rourke says.

"I don't know about the man, but the girl's name should be in the file."

"We're way ahead of you, Flannery," O'Shea says. "Ain't we way ahead of him, Rourke?"

"It's the next stop," Rourke says. "You want to come along with us? It'll save us all asking the same questions."

I glance over at Mary Ellen Dunne, who is staring at her hands as though surprised to see them on the ends of her wrists.

"The precinct captain don't want to do the donkey work," O'Shea says. "He's a public-relations man. He's a vote-getter."

"I could go with you, O'Shea," my father says.

"Like hell. Neither one of you is official. I'll maybe stretch a point for Delvin's man, but I ain't taking along a crowd."

"So, I'll wait in the corner saloon," my old man says, "and when you get done talking to the girl and her grandmother, or whoever, you come by and I'll buy you a beer."

"Ah, Jesus," O'Shea says disgustedly, "the heavy bribes I get offered me." He walks away, followed by Rourke, who gives Mike the friendly thumbs-up as he follows his partner.

My old man tells me to go ahead and take the nurse to the hospital. "Ask her is she Irish." No matter what else, my unmarried condition distresses Mike. Even when we go to funerals, he's casing the church looking for a likely.

Once he practically tucked me into bed with Bridget Monahan, who was promised to Jesus, after the wedding of her sister, Kate. I was a little drunk but she was not, and that saved us both. Bridget became a nun and went away for three years. Then she quit and came back to Chicago, where she took up the study of the law. She's down in City Hall working for the public defender. She has a reputation for being sweet and tough.

When she sees me, she likes to tease and tells me that after lying on the covers with me—even though we was fully dressed—she couldn't stand the convent. I'd ruined her for Christ, she says, but she don't really mean it. She has a boyfriend who is some kind of Latin and they go to church every morning and twice on Sundays.

In my car, Mary Ellen Dunne sighs like a tired child and puts her head on my shoulder like we know each other twenty years. Her hair has red glints in the brown. I think about a fireplace and wish I had one in my flat.

"Mary Ellen Dunne . . ." I says.

"Hush. Please, hush," she says.

I don't say another word and she don't move her head. We get to Passavant. She gets out of the car without waiting for me to open the door. I lock up and follow her up the gray stone steps. Inside the lobby, she turns right and I follow her down the corridor to the coffee shop. She puts her palm out to warn me off. So I sit at a table while she goes to the counter and brings back two coffees and two sweet rolls.

"So, all right, James Flannery, ask me what you want to know."

"How do you know my name?"

"Your father told me. He told me how you're the man to see for favors in the precinct, and that you're a comer. He told me that you like cats and barley soup. He told me your mother died of cancer eight years ago."

"Did he tell you she was the person in the family who called me James?"

"No, he didn't tell me that. So, did I do something good?"

"What do you mean?"

"Not every man wants to marry a woman like his mother."

Then she smiles and I see she's pulling my leg . . . and I don't mind.

"That why you got cozy with me in the car?" I kid her back. "Was you setting your cap for me?"

The smile goes away and the sunshine leaves her face. "No, James, I put my head on your shoulder for the reason I told you. I was sick and tired of so much that's awful, and you smelled of lemon soap and clean linen."

"Tell me how it went."

"Do you know anything about the routine?"

"The doctor explained . . ."

"Chapman."

"Doctor Chapman gave me the drill from his point of view."

"He left the examining room."

"So you were talking to the girl . . ."

"Young woman."

"You were explaining what was going to happen . . ."

"I explained it, and told her to go into the operating room."

"The next room."

"Not exactly the next room. There's no connecting door. You have to go out one door and into the next. The clinic was a chicken market. One big room and a meat locker. We hammered up some partitions and tried to make a plan that would give the patients as much privacy as we could."

"Chapman said he waited in the office for the knock that told him the next patient was ready for him."

"The doctor's office is over on the other side of the operating room. It's the only one that has a door that connects with another room. In fact, the operating room is the only one that has two doors. One to the corridor and one to the outside."

She sees that I'm lost and draws a floor plan of the clinic on a napkin. Then I've got it.

"So you show the young woman the door to the operating room and . . ."

"No, I leave first while she takes a minute. Sometimes they want me to hold their hand all the way. Sometimes they want to be left alone for a minute before going into the room where their baby is going to be taken from them. Sometimes they even decide not to go through with it."

"What do you do next?"

"I go to get the information on the next patient, if there is one."

"And there is one. She's with an older woman."

"Yes. But I didn't go to them right away."

"Why not?"

"There was a man in the corridor. I asked him what he was doing there. He showed me a badge and said he was sent to make sure Joe Asbach and the Right-to-Lifers didn't make any more trouble."

That is a favor I owe Pescaro. He might have been keeping an eye out anyway, but I figure the man inside is a special favor he done for me after I take him the knife and explain my concern.

"Is this the skinny man with thinning hair?" I says.

"No. This a tall, good-looking man with black hair combed like Rudolph Valentino."

"What is Mrs. Klutzman doing in the operating room? She ain't a nurse."

"She's the best kind of nurse," Mary Ellen Dunne says, "but I know what you mean. Rose . . ."

"That's her name?"

". . . was the best aide I ever knew," she says, nodding her head.

"I never knew her first name."

"Even the professionals at Passavant are not as good as she is."

"So, please, was she always in the operating room when the patient walked in?" I says.

"I don't know about that. Somtimes, I suppose. But she didn't have to be. We worked so well together that it wasn't often the doctor or I had to tell her what to do or where to be. She just did what needed doing."

"I'm just trying to figure was she there when the girl walked in after the examination, or did she walk in after the girl was already in it."

"I can't help you there. I don't know."

"Did any of the demonstrators come in?"

"I don't know that either. Anybody could come in. With just a little luck, nobody would even see them, I suppose."

"Was there anything else—any threat—besides the knife and the ketchup?"

"There was something," Mary Ellen Dunne says. "Monday night I go home from work and my cat is lying dead on my doorstep with its head cut off."

After Mary Ellen Dunne stops crying, she gets me the number of Mrs. Klutzman's room, but when I get there, Mrs. Klutzman is dead.

I ask Mary Ellen Dunne does she want to ask for the night off and I'll see her home.

"Death is a thing that happens in the work I do," she says.

"I know, but Rose was a friend," I says.

"That's why I'm going to work my shift."

Back at my place on Polk Street, I climb the six flights to the door of my flat like I'm a hundred and six years old. There's two more flights up to the roof. From there you can look out across the city in practically every direction except east, where there's another apartment building taller than the one that I live in. I hesitate at the bottom of the first flight, wondering if I can make it, but wanting a look at the sky so bad I can feel it tugging at my belly.

I climb the stairs and push open the metal-clad door. The hinges and springs screech like a woman with a hand over her mouth.

There's a wood railing all around.

The roof is laid with tar which bubbles in the summer. I played on such roofs all my life, even when we lived in a one-family house. After the sun went down and the bubbles hardened, my friends and me would bust them with ice-cream sticks.

The housewives hung out their clothes to dry on the roofs. There was catwalks built so they wouldn't damage the tar under the paths where the lines was strung. Most of the younger women take their stuff to the laundromat nowadays, but Mrs. Warnowski still does her wash in an old Maytag with an electric wringer and hangs it on the roof. She probably doesn't know it, but on summer days, I come up to the roof and bury my face in her clean sheets. Sun has a smell. Most people forget that, or never knew it.

At night it's a place I go like women and old men go to church.

There's somebody else up on the roof leaning on the rail. At first I think it's somebody who lives in the house, but when I get closer I see it's my old man.

"What are you doing here this time of night?" I says.

"Checking up on you to see if you was coming

home late or coming home at all," he says. "Is she Irish?"

"I didn't ask."

"I don't think she's Irish, but I think she's a very nice girl," he says.

I can see his concern for his unmarried son is getting very bad if he's touting a filly who might have foreign bloodlines.

"Did O'Shea come back for his beer?"

"Oh, sure, they both come. He's all right. Just he grew his skin too thick."

"Rourke's a sweetheart."

"Yes, he is, but I think it would be a toss-up which cares the most."

"What about the girl in the waiting room and her . . ."

". . . friend. The old woman was a neighbor. The girl's got no family here."

"They see the skinny guy?"

"Their backs was to the door."

"How about the cop?"

Mike shakes his head.

"So he must have come in the side door through the doctor's office."

We stand there leaning on the rail, looking out over the city.

"God works in mysterious ways," my old man says.

I feel a twinge over my heart. I realize how old my father's getting and how he could be turning to God the way people do when they can see death waiting for them, not too far away, down there in the fog at the bottom of the road.

"The girl's going back to her hometown and have the baby," he says. "So there was that much good come of it."

"It's mysterious like you say, but I don't know if two, maybe three for one is a very Christian bargain."

6

I go up the outside back stairs of the six-family where Mrs. Klutzman lived. There's a big tree with its top right where it blocks the morning light from Mrs. Klutzman's kitchen window. I remembered the last time I sat at the table by the window having a bagel and a cup of tea with Mrs. Klutzman, whose name I didn't know was Rose.

"Mr. Flannery, could you do for me a favor?"

"That's what I'm here for, Mrs. Klutzman."

"You could maybe talk to whoever and ask them would they trim that big limb off the tree outside this window? You can see how it steals the sun. Get as old as me and the sun on the bones is as good as a sirloin steak, which I cannot afford and probably could not digest even if I could afford it, in the belly."

"I'll put a word in the right ear."

"You're a good boy."

That was quite a while ago when she asked me to have it trimmed and I forgot to do the favor for the first time in I don't know when. She only asked me the one time. People who don't complain, don't get remembered, I'm sorry to say.

The kitchen door to the porch is open even though the leaves are turning yellow and it's getting cold. An old man hands me a paper yarmulke, but I ask him is it all right I wear my crushed tweed hat.

"You want you should look like an Irisher in a

34

kosher house, so what difference is that to God?" he says sweetly.

There's no furniture in the house, which is the way the Orthodox do when they are sitting *shiva*. They take out all the furniture and wear old clothes and put ashes on their faces and breasts. They sit on orange crates. Lately they sit on plastic milk crates or cardboard boxes. Who makes from wood anymore?

I don't know everyone, but nearly everyone, in the parlor. Joe Pakula is there with his mother and his sister, Pearl. He comes over and takes my hand in his hand. He looks like a Spanish saint.

"It's cold in here," I says.

"So, we should feel the cold and know our fate," he says, and leads me to a Coca-Cola carton.

I sit there feeling foolish and sad. The Jews know how to make a person feel humble in the presence of death.

Mrs. Klutzman is wrapped in a white sheet. Even her neck, cheeks, and hair are wound in it. I can only see her hands, which look like wax, and her dry lips and her nose, sharp like a knife, sticking up. She is laying on a plank set on two chairs.

It's all very old-fashioned. Modern times ain't caught up with a good many people who live in the Twenty-seventh. Somehow I like them better for it.

Joe Pakula puts his hand on my sleeve and leans over to whisper in my ear. "The Irish drink at these affairs, don't they?" he says.

It's in all the papers, but it ain't *all* in the papers.

The *Tribune* has a one-column head, first page, that says "Explosion at Abortion Clinic." Three inches tells the public that a woman seeking an abortion was killed in the explosion of what appeared to be a faulty gas connection . . . "though the remote possibility that it was planned and not a case of misadventure is being investigated by police, firemen, and city building inspectors."

The *Sun-Times* don't even give it that much on the third page.

The death of Mrs. Klutzman ain't mentioned because she dies after they go to press. The next day there will be a little obit, but no story to go with it linking her death to the clinic.

There's no mention of a bomb in either paper, either day. Who's being cautious? *Why's* somebody being cautious?

Mary Ellen Dunne says, "Are we having a date . . ."

It's Friday morning. The early light is like dishwater on the bricks outside the diner window across from Passavant. I'm having ham and eggs. She's having hot cereal and milk.

". . . or are you going to ask me more questions?"

"I expected to see you over to Mrs. Klutzman's last night," I says.

"I meant to be there."

"Dead before morning, they bury before nightfall."

"I know. I was ready to go, but I felt so many tears here"—she tapped herself between her breasts—"I knew I'd drown if I went."

"It's okay. I don't think anybody expected . . . Only old people and a few neighbors were there."

"Doctor Chapman?"

"Yes, he was there. He come in while I was leaving."

"He knew the customs. Figures. He'd make it his business to know such things."

"You like him?"

"What's not to like? So, you haven't answered me. Is this a date?"

"You want it to be a date?" I says.

She eyes me for a minute like I'm getting used to, and then she smiles. "If this is a date, buy me a piece of peach pie."

*   *   *

The dead girl's name is Helen Addison, it says on the records in the clinic files that have escaped the blast and fire. I write down the name and the address she gave. Badger Street is in the neighborhood.

Chapman sits there in his office wearing a sports jacket and topcoat looking like a high-class bookie without his granny glasses.

"What are you doing?" he says. "What do you expect to find?"

"I just like to go over and pay my respects. I take care of these people."

"You didn't take care of a couple of them very well."

"That sonofabitch Joe Asbach is a hun from outside the district. He gets himself a license to march in my neighborhood. He didn't get it from me."

"You're not going to find anyone by that name ever lived at that address," he says.

"Don't I know that?" I says, "She's laying down there in the morgue unclaimed . . ."

"Practically none of them give a real name and address," he says.

". . . but she wrote down an address she might have been familiar with," I says. "She maybe gave the name of a friend. Most people ain't very good at making things up."

"Well, I don't think this one would . . ."

He fumbles in his pocket and takes out the granny glasses. When he puts them on, I don't know if they make him look meaner or milder.

"Would what?"

"Have any trouble making things up."

"You got to translate. How come you say that from just looking her over?"

"I think she was a professional. New to it, maybe, but there were signs."

"Why did you hesitate about saying that?"

"I don't know. How can I be sure you won't attack me for saying something disrespectful about a white girl?"

"Is it still that bad for you out there?"

"It's that bad," he says. "They going to pick up this Asbach?"

"I'm going to find out why they haven't got him in the slam already. Why you sitting around here?"

"We're going to clean this place up," he says. "People like Asbach aren't going to drive us out."

"Ain't you got volunteers who can do the dirty work?"

"Everything's dirty work," he says, "and nothing's dirty work."

"The girl who was waiting her turn . . ."

"The last one scheduled . . . ?"

". . . and the old lady who was a friend what was with her didn't see the cop Mary Ellen Dunne saw in the corridor."

"That's not hard to understand."

"That would mean he didn't pass through the waiting room."

Chapman stared at my throat as though that was the spot where he was planning to put the knife.

"Which would mean he got into the building through your office and got out the same way."

Chapman stood up. For a second I thought he was going to take a swing at me. Then he turns around and makes his way through the rubble like a soldier on parade. "Follow me," he says.

I follow him into the corridor and down another hall to the back where there's a door marked MEN. He pushes it open and I follow him into a room with two urinals, a toilet in a cabinet, and a cracked tile floor. It's very cold. There's an open window big enough to let a big man pass through and a heavy pipe halfway up the wall that could be used for a step.

* * *

The Department of Streets and Sanitation has a bunch of offices where you could get lost even if you know your way around. The trick is to find Wally Dunleavy's, which is in the middle of the floor with a single window facing an air shaft like he wasn't one of the most powerful patronage bosses in the city. He ain't even got an outer office or a secretary to keep people out.

When I walk in, he looks up from a street map, which he is working on with a ruler and a red pen, and says, "You're Mike Flannery's kid."

"Yes, I am, Mr. Dunleavy."

"You look just like him. I got an eye."

"You also got a memory. My father says he ain't seen you in fifteen years."

"More like sixteen, but who's counting, right? Sit down. Sit down."

I move some books off the one other chair in the office, which is as big as a broom closet and stuffed with rolled-up maps from one end to the other, and wait for him to do the rest of his act, even though I know he's been finding out about me from the minute I stepped through the first door into his department. By the time I made the first turning, somebody had me identified by name. By the second, my pedigree was out of the files. By the third, memories of my old man had already been dredged up from somebody's head and delivered to Dunleavy.

Rumor has it that he saw his wife-to-be at the end of a reception hall at a party for Monseigneur Flynn, decided he would marry her, and by the time she walked the length of the floor, had found out her age, place of birth, and blood type. It's his talent.

"You're interested in parades and demonstrations," he says. "You're interested in a particular demonstration."

"The one at the abortion clinic over to Sperry."

"Don't tell me, I'll tell you." He grins, making red lines on the map, probably chopping up a corner of the city for some stadium or public building, displacing hundreds, maybe thousands of people.

"This Joe Asbach . . . yes, we gave him a permit. How could we do otherwise?"

"You know just about everything that goes on in the streets, Mr. Dunleavy. Did you know about the knife?"

"With the ketchup?"

"And the cat?"

"Without a head?"

"So you know about these things."

"And I don't pull his permit. That's right. I've got no probable cause. This is a free country. This is a free city."

I think about the cops clubbing citizens in the streets back in 1968.

"I just wondered if there was anybody else put in a good word for Asbach?"

"Half the aldermen in the city put in a good word for Asbach. Why shouldn't they? Ain't he on the side of the angels?"

Captain Pescaro is unconcerned.

"Are you making an effort over this Asbach?" I says.

"Hold your water, Flannery," he says. "Every day that fool stays under cover makes the case against him."

"Has Missing Persons turned anything on the dead girl?"

"Not a thing. Her description's out. Her finger-prints are being circulated. One will get you five she ain't born and bred in Chicago. You got to understand she's not top priority."

"That's why I'm taking an interest," I says.

"How big is your interest?"

"She's a person who was killed in my precinct."

"A visitor."

"That don't matter. She was in my house. It has to do with the honor of my house."

"I can understand that," he says. "This is my mansion, too."

"You got a picture?"

He opens up the top drawer of his desk and thumbs open a manila file. He plucks out a forensic photo which they took after they washed her face. He hands it to me and says, "I shouldn't."

"Is this a big favor or a little one?"

"It's on the house. Anybody asks you where you got that, it wasn't from me."

I walk out wondering why, if this unidentified body ain't top priority, Pescaro's got her file in his desk.

7

I go over to Badger Street. There's an empty lot
where 208 should be. Two three-story frames are on
each side of a lot the neighborhood is using for
dumping trash. A rusty bedspring is sticking up curly
fingers. A refrigerator is laying on its side with its
mouth open like a dead giant. Somebody has bal-
anced ten worn tires in a pile. It looks like modern
art. I think if I put a railing around it maybe I can
get one of the culture mavens should give me a
grant.

The junk is at least as interesting as the thing
Picasso gives the city down at Daley Center Plaza,
which nobody can tell what it is with its steely eyes—a
bird, a dog, or a Chicago lawyer.

While I'm looking, this one slides in behind me. I
stick my hand on my wallet and take a long step
before turning around in case whoever it is means to
clout me from behind.

He looks like a crane, wearing red moss for a
sweater, with its nest on its head.

"I piled them tires," he says.

"They are beauties."

"My art is not much appreciated."

"It takes time."

"It used to be you could shoot yourself in the leg
and get in *People* and on *Face the Nation*."

"Them was the good old days."

"That guy who wired his balls to the house current

42

and that lady who played the cello with her bare tits hanging out ruined it for everybody."

"There's always somebody will go too damn far," I says.

Now that we're agreed on the state of the avant garde, I show him the picture.

"That's Helen," he says.

"You know her?"

"I met her when she first come to Chicago. I buy her a coffee when she arrives on the Greyhound. I spend a lot of time at the Greyhound."

"Any particular reason?"

"The train station is too big and the airport is too far."

From the way he tells me, I'm supposed to know what that means, so I act like I do. Otherwise he'll no longer look on me as a soul brother.

"You wait to get lucky, like with Helen?"

"Oh, no, I wait for a three-bus crash."

"You pick Helen up?"

He looks down at his tatters as though he knows I'm saying I can't understand why a young woman should walk up to a man who looks like a ragbag.

"These is my work clothes," he says. "When I hang around the Greyhound, I wear my best. This Helen walks up to me thinking I'm a pimp out recruiting. She ain't been the only one."

"But you ain't a pimp."

"Well ..." he says, not wanting to give up the momentary shine the idea of being a ladies' man gives him.

"If you was a pimp around here, my man, I would know it," I says.

He laughs, showing big yellow teeth like a horse.

"You're cop," he says. "You fooled me. Usually I smell them."

"So did you steer her?" I says.

"Oh, no, I buy her a coffee and tell her she should go home."

"But she don't want to."

"That's right. None of them want to. They think a big city is a palace of wonders. I tell her Chicago ain't nothing like that. But she says she won't leave, and I take her home so she's got a place to sleep for the night without spending what little money she's got."

"You're a Good Samaritan."

"I know my bible," he says, "but I don't do charity."

"You live next door?"

"No, I live down the block. I look for empty lots. Empty lots is my canvases."

"How long did she stay?"

"A week, maybe two."

"How long ago?"

"A year and a half. It was spring."

"And after the week, maybe two?"

"She got her own place."

"You know where?"

He shakes his head and grins like a fool.

"She says she don't want me to know because I'm a man what is like candy and she's afraid I'll come bother her and take her mind off her purpose."

"So that's the last you see her?"

"Oh, no, she comes to me when she wants a taste."

He's telling me what a sweet man he is, catnip for the ladies. I know they say love is blind, but there should be limits. I know he's really telling me that he and Helen tooted up a little.

"What's your name, by the way?" I says.

"Bo Addison," he says.

"She ever tell you her name?"

"Said it was Marshall, but it weren't."

"How do you know?"

"I saw a name and address on a letter she had in her purse."

"What was the name?"

"Caplet."

"What was the address?"

"General Delivery."

Mary Ellen Dunne's flat is small, but like a picture out of a magazine. She's done like they do to pine furniture and streaked it with white, so it shines in the light of the factory lamps overhead, which she's covered with colored scarves. There's a daybed under the louvered windows with a pile of pillows looking like little flower beds on it.

A table is set with pottery and candles. There's only two wooden chairs.

There's a chest of drawers she calls a chiffonier against one wall, with a jelly jar on it filled with weeds arranged like cut flowers.

There's also an old-fashioned picture of a bride and a groom. The man's wearing a top hat, the woman's wearing a veil down her back with a circle of flowers holding it around her head. They're dark-skinned and dark-eyed.

"That was taken the day my folks broke the glass under the arbor," she says. "They're Hebes, I guess you can tell."

"You shouldn't use a word like that," I says. "It's an insult."

"Not when a Jew says it. It's like a black calling another black a motherfucker."

She's standing there staring at me, looking for signs. I stare right back. People who give you surprises like that think they can read the truth of your feelings in your eyes. They spring the trap and act like it's no more than they had a right to expect of a bigot if you say ouch.

"Where'd you get Dunne?" I says.

"I was married to a man of that name. It lasted a year."

"Culture shock?"

"You might say. A drunk driver hit him when he stepped off the curb on his way to work. That was two years ago."

"Your looks and your name didn't fool my father. He asked me to ask was you Irish."

"There goes my chance to infiltrate his family," she says.

"Your mouth is very pretty most of the time," I says. "It's not very pretty when you're being flip."

"If you expect me to ask you into my bedroom, forget it." She waves a hand at the daybed. "This is it."

"Are you hungry?" Mary Ellen says.

I'm too full of the good things we did together in her daybed to answer, but I grunt to let her know I'm not the sort to fall asleep right after. She props herself up and leans over me. Her breasts are like apples. She touches my chest with them. I know she's staring into my face in the nicest way.

"I *was* hungry," Mary Ellen says, meaning for loving.

"Me, too. I was hungry, too," I says, meaning the same.

"Don't kid me," she says. "You're the kind women make offers."

I open my eyes. Her face don't know whether to be serious or wise-guy.

"How come you look like you look?" I says.

"My mother had three kids with my father. They all died or got killed one way or another. She was forty and he was fifty. He got the mumps and it made him sterile. He couldn't help her have another. They had a friend . . ."

"You don't have to tell me," I says. "It's none of my business."

"Unless what we just did was good-bye," she says, "I want to tell you. I think it's a beautiful story, no matter what anybody else might think. The friend's name was Bannion. My mother and father had a talk. She told me it went on nonstop for twenty hours. They reached an agreement based on needs, wants, and love. My mother and Bannion went to the country for the weekend. Just one weekend. It was the right time of the month. For the next three weeks he stayed near enough for her to call. When she did, he said he had plans to go to Cleveland. They never saw one another again. My father subscribed to the Cleveland newspapers. Just before he died himself, he saw the obituary on Bannion. I lost two fathers in the same year."

"Your mother?"

"She lives over in Mount Prospect with my aunt, her sister. They keep a kosher house, but you don't have to worry, I have bacon with my eggs. I'm half Irish. So your father's half right and I'm half lucky."

"What does that mean?"

"So maybe I can't be a good Irishman's wife, but maybe I can be his girlfriend," she says, twisting her face like she's kidding.

She's falling back on funny because it's always painful to expose your heart.

"That's a beautiful story you tell about your mother, your father, and Bannion," I says, "and, now, can we eat?"

8

"Her name is Helen Caplet," I says, tossing a card on which I wrote her name in front of Pescaro.

He eyes me, nods, opens the desk drawer, and tosses the card on top of the file.

The door opens up at my back and one of his detectives sticks his head in. "Excuse, Captain . . ." he says.

Pescaro starts making a face like he's got indigestion . . .

". . . Asbach's hollering to see a lawyer."

. . . but not in time. The beans is spilled.

"You were going to keep me informed," I says.

"Oh, no," he says, "that favor wasn't asked and wasn't given."

"I would like to speak to the man. I would like to remind him of a conversation we had."

"Benedetto, you take Flannery to see Asbach. You give him five minutes . . ."

"It won't even take that long," I says.

". . . and you stay in the room with him," Pescaro says.

"Yes, Captain."

"When you get done, Flannery, I want you should come back for a minute."

Benedetto takes me to the interrogation room, where Asbach is sitting looking brave. Asbach looks up at me, then looks at Benedetto. He's trying to figure out the connection. He's trying to figure out how much juice I got.

I look at Benedetto.

"I just want to have a private word," I says.

"You heard the captain."

"You do everything you're told to do?"

"Favor for favor?"

"I know the rules."

Benedetto starts closing the door. "You want to do damage, do it quiet. I got to have an alibi and I ain't deaf," he says.

I stand staring down on Asbach. When he doesn't stand up I know I got the power.

"You know me?" I says.

"You're the shoeshine boy that goes around making his own business," he says.

"I don't see how you can be so smart with two people dead. Three, you count the baby you're so hot to protect. Murder to prevent murder, that's a funny way."

"I didn't lay that bomb," Asbach says. "I was nowhere around. I have witnesses."

"It maybe wasn't your hand actually put the bomb, laid the knife, and cut off the cat's head, but your hand was in it. The book the judge is going to throw at you is being printed right now. You think this is Bean Town? You think this is New York? You make a mess in Chicago, you clean it up with your tongue."

His face crumples up like a piece of tissue paper all of a sudden. "Listen," he says, "I didn't do any of these things. I didn't order them done . . ."

"You did the knife. You knew all about the knife . . ."

"Oh, yes, the knife. I did the knife and the ketchup. It was a symbol."

"It was a threat."

"It was a sign, for Christ's sake."

"Don't bring Him into it. You got no right. Don't try to cop a plea with me. You're the guy who said in the New York papers that you don't put down bombers and arsonists."

"I said I didn't support them."

"No, you just said, 'What's a little damaged real estate . . . It's like bombing Dachau and not hurting anyone.' "

He reaches out and grabs my sleeve. I don't jerk away. I let him hold on. I'm going to let him try to persuade me.

"You did the cat," I says.

"God as my witness . . ."

"You going to call on the whole family?"

". . . I didn't cut off that cat's head."

"How come you know about that too? Was it in the papers? Was it printed on a wall?"

"It could be one of the new members who joined up last week who did it," he says.

"Give me a name."

"I haven't got it in my head. You understand? I can't remember the name of every new member who signs up."

"It's written down?"

"I'll get the list as soon as I can get to it."

"All right, I hear you," I says. "Now you can let me go."

Captain Pescaro is waiting for me in his office.

"I'm back," I says.

"I can see," he says. "Don't bother sitting down. This won't take long. You did good getting the girl's name . . ."

He doesn't ask me how I get it.

". . . so now let us officers of the law do what we get paid for. It's all right you should take care of your people; it's not all right you should be a cop."

"Is that it?" I says.

"That's all I've got to say. But I'm also asked to tell you that you're wanted for a conversation over to your master's office."

"What is this 'master' business?"

"Well, you're Delvin's dog, ain't you?"

* * *

I hear Delvin called "avuncular" once. It sounded like it fit him. Then somebody tells me it means like an uncle. I thought "avuncular" had something to do with elephants.

It's not so much he's fat. It's more like the way his skin hangs around his collar, the folds of flesh bluish-gray from always needing a shave. It's the way his pants bag over his shoes and sag at the crotch. It's the way his eyes are always weeping.

"You don't touch base with me lately, Jimbo," he says, wiping his eyes with a white hankie.

"I don't have nothing needs your attention."

"Everything can use my attention. Everything in your precinct needs *your* attention, and everything in my ward can use *my* attention. I don't see you since the last time you run a little errand for me."

"For which I was grateful to have the chance to do."

"I know that. Ain't your old man and me been friends for fifty years? Ain't I the guy who took you out of the sewers?"

I don't mention that he's also the man who put me *in* the sewers.

"So, have you got any troubles could use my ear?" he says.

"I wish I could say there was. You've got this ward running so smooth, you must go crazy sitting around with nothing to do except just listening to it hum."

He wipes his eyes and they go like from twinkly to mean. Delvin wants to be the only one who spreads the chicken fat. I'm about to fall in the shit, and if I don't watch out, I'll be swimming upstream.

"A friend of mine got killed," I says.

"One of our constituents?" he says.

"A good Democrat who voted the straight ticket."

"You send flowers?"

"No."

"Now, you see, there? You should have sent flowers. You should have sent flowers from me and the party."

"Mrs. Klutzman was Hebrew Orthodox. There wasn't any flowers."

"This is the old lady who was blown to pieces?" he says, nodding like the wise old elephant I once thought he was called.

"You know about her?"

"Why would I not know about somebody dies by violence in the Twenty-seventh, Jimbo? It's like you should ask me would I know if there's a corpse in my parlor."

"I did what I could. She had nobody."

"There was also a young woman. Helen Caplet."

"You know about her, too?" I says.

He wipes his weeping eyes. "Oh, yes, I know all about the poor misguided girl who was foolish enough to be in such a place when some overzealous Christian made a miscalculation."

" 'Miscalculation'?"

"Well, you don't suppose anybody was trying to kill a pregnant waif, do you? You don't suppose somebody had it in for a nice old Jewish grandmother?"

"Somebody cut the head off the cat which belonged to the nurse who works in the clinic part-time," I says.

"A cat is not a person, is it, Jim?" he says. He's dropped the "Jimbo" and is being avuncular. "We got to keep these things in perspective. Now, let this matter rest. Go on to other things. And, remember, I'm always here to help."

"On the subject," I says, "maybe you can help me with the case of the widow of a fireman named Warnowski who . . ."

". . . was drunk . . ."

". . . was a loyal employee of the city for one month short of thirty years . . ."

". . . and wrecked his goddamn car and busted a light pole."

". . . and died trying to avoid a cat in the road."

"Who says so?"

"There was a witness," I says.

"I didn't know that."

"Even a man who knows everything can't know everything. Not about a thing like a cat, begging your pardon," I says.

"So what do you want?"

"Full pension for his widow."

"Well, I don't know. Where do you draw the line? A man dies thirty days before full retirement, and you make an exception, so the next thing you know another man leaves forty-five days, maybe sixty days before retirement. Maybe ninety. Who's got the case? Does everybody got a case? Besides, Warnowski was a drunk."

"I don't know if that's written down anywhere."

"But he was a drunk?"

I don't confirm or deny.

"You know how the citizens is up in arms about drunk drivers these days."

"As well they should be," I says.

"Well, then," Delvin says, as though that is his entire winning argument.

"Warnowski comes out of the Polish working class, like you and me come out of the Irish working class," I says. "What did we grow up with? A man was expected to be a heavy drinker. If he was a heavy drinker, as long as he don't beat the wife or neglect the kids, everybody says, 'Old Stash, old Paddy, can really put it away, but he never beats the wife, he never neglects the kids, and he never misses a day's work because of the drink."

"You got a sweet tongue, Jimbo. My God, you're Irish."

So old legends about what the Irish are like, and the Jews are like, and the blacks are like, just keep on rolling along, because I don't want to have a discussion about stereotypes; I just want to win my cause.

"Well," Delvin says, "I mean, thirty days. What's thirty days?"

"Four weeks," I says.

"One month," Delvin says.

So we now got it down to a practical minute.

"All right," Delvin says, "I see what I can do."

"And maybe a citation?"

"A what?"

"Not a medal, but maybe just a little citation signed by his grand ward leader."

"How the hell do we get to where we're honoring the sonofabitch?"

"He kept a police radio in his car. He could've heard a call and was rushing to the firehouse to do his duty even though it was his day off," I says.

Delvin looks at me with real admiration. "By Christ, Jimbo," he says, "you can sure pile it high."

I found out from some back copies of the Chicago *Tribune* that Asbach's staying at the Essex House Hotel. I go over there and find Harry Chickering, who is the house detective.

"Do you want my marker?" I says.

"I'd rather have fifty bucks," Chickering says. "But that depends."

"On what?"

"On the favor you want for me to do you."

"I want to get into a room."

"Not to steal?"

I don't even bother to answer. There's not a soul in the city who knows me who doesn't know I wouldn't steal a pin. I hand him a folded twenty.

"Give me the key and the number. The name is Joe Asbach."

Chickering has no faith. He unfolds the bill.

"I don't want to buy the room," I says. "I just want to look at it."

"Three-oh-five. I'll take the twenty, but I've got half a marker on you."

Chickering is the kind who always collects a little extra. How do you call in half a marker?

I go into Asbach's room. He's a very neat person. His papers are all tucked away in a briefcase that opens up into an expandable file. I find his Chicago membership list. It's typed out except for three names at the bottom. Two of them are women. The other is a man named Gino Ciccone who lives on the West Side in Vito Velletri's Twenty-fifth.

The phone rings and I lift it up.

"Asbach's on his way up," Chickering tells me. "Now you owe me a full marker."

I'm standing in front of the elevator when the door opens and Asbach steps out. At first he looks startled, then self-satisfied.

"I come to get that name," I says. "I heard you was out on bail."

"Well, you can whistle for it," he says. "I'm not out on bail. I'm out clean."

"The cops believed your alibi? They believed your witnesses?"

"There's no case against me."

"Are these witnesses anyone I maybe would know?"

"The witness is a young lady I doubt you would ever have occasion to meet."

"Are you staying in town?"

"Maybe I'll stay, maybe I'll go. I'm a respectable citizen with the right to come and go as I please. The police didn't even warn me about leaving town."

"Then I hope you're staying," I says, "because it ain't over with us."

"Oh, yes it is. You're so dumb you don't know enough to fall down and roll over when you've been shot."

9

I've got no appetite for Dan Blatna's kielbasa and cabbage.

"Are you in love?" my old man says.

I jump like he stuck me with a hot nail. It's only just that minute I think maybe that Mary Ellen is more to me in one night than any other woman's ever been to me in a month of Sundays.

"I got a little heartburn," I says.

He grins into his cabbage. "She's not Irish, is she?" he says.

"You got an eye like an eagle."

"So, what is she?"

I don't want to tell even my old man the story, not because it would put a mark on Mary Ellen, but because you tell a story to me and I take it with me to the grave unless you say otherwise.

So I only says, "She is half and half."

"What's the other half?"

"Hebrew."

"Well, all Irish or not, I know the right goods when I see it. Now that you know what I already knew, you can eat."

He's right. My appetite comes back. Also I start thinking about other things except the funny feeling that was fooling around my heart which I thought was indigestion but which I now find out is love.

"You'll do something for me?" I says.

"Favor for favor?"

"Whatever," I says.

"Ask me."

"You know every fireman in the city?"

"It was my calling."

"Will you ask the boys at the firehouse what answered the alarm to the clinic what kind of bomb it was? How big? Where it was planted?"

"Why don't you ask them? Only one company rolled on that one, and it's in your precinct."

I'm not all that quick to answer.

"It's that way, is it?" my old man says. "Who's doing the stone-walling?"

"Delvin called me in for a talk."

My old man is thoughtful.

"Joe Asbach walked out of the police station without a leash," I says. "He's home free and there's not even a good beginning to the investigation yet."

"You know what it could be? It could be Delvin don't like what they do at that clinic so he gives this Asbach a pass."

"I don't like it either, but I don't think it's any of my business. Neither do I think it's any of Delvin's. One way or the other way, though, nobody should get away with setting a bomb."

"Delvin ain't got any kids of his own. He's got a soft heart for kids. When you was little, every time he sees you he gives you a quarter."

"He laid the foundation of my fortune," I says.

"Don't crack wise with your old man when he's giving you reasons why."

I fold my hands and look polite like I did at the table just before Sunday dinner while my mother— God love and keep her soul—said grace.

"Maybe Old Man Delvin thinks about it and sees every one of them little kids what will not get born like it could be one of his own kids that never was."

"The way the story goes, it was his own fault he's got no kids."

My old man looks at me like he used to look at me

when I did something to break his heart with disappointment when I was growing up. He never had to look that way often, and he ain't looked at me that way in years.

"Bite your tongue, Jim," he says. "This ain't the charity I taught you to hold in your heart. There's not a human being alive who ain't made a mistake or two every day of his or her life. Most mistakes ain't much—you get over them quick—but some mistakes you got to pay off forever."

"Does that mean Delvin does penance by turning his head when somebody tries to close down an abortion clinic the way they done?"

"No. Wrong is wrong, no matter who does it. I'm saying if Delvin called you off it's because he knows—"

" 'Called me off?' " I nearly shout.

"—things you maybe don't have to know . . ."

"I ain't a dog. Two people is dead," I says. "That is a mistake I think somebody should pay for."

"You're damned right. I'm just saying, for the minute, give your boss the benefit of the doubt and show him a little trust and loyalty."

"Are we talking one good house dog to another?" I says.

My old man gets quiet all over. It's something he does like a cat arches its back. His eyes look so blue I expect little bolts of lightning to flash out and hit me between the eyes.

"I was never anybody's house dog," he says. "I was *the* mayor's man. I was never *a* mayor's man. I was never Daley's man. I don't want you should be a dog. I do want you should be loyal."

After the speech, he sticks his fork in a sausage.

"There's maybe another thing to this," I says.

"What that?"

"Maybe Delvin, maybe somebody else, maybe several somebodies, has relations with that girl, Helen Caplet. Maybe they pass her around like they pass around the name of a new restaurant what just opened up. Maybe she plays with a good many big men and maybe she's got ambitions. Maybe she's using the games what she plays with these old men for a handle to put on the squeeze. Maybe the abortion is part of a blackmail payoff."

"And maybe you want to change human nature," Mike says, like he wants to snap my head off.

"This dinner's on me," I says.

"You don't got to buy me. I ain't going to stay offended."

"I just want to pay for good advice."

"In that case I'll have another whiskey."

After a minute I says, "You don't mind talking to the firemen? Just to satisfy the old curiosity?"

"It won't hurt," my old man says.

10

"You're petting me like I'm a cat," Mary Ellen says. "Any minute I'm going to purr."

"You got skin like kid leather," I says.

"So, now I'm a glove," she says, teasing me.

"Oh, Mary Ellen," I says, taking her hand, "you're the whole outfit."

"You're a sweet-talking sonofabitch," she says.

"Hey, don't use that expression," I says.

"Oh, James, it wasn't meant."

"I know that. It's just that people get so careless the way they use words."

She lays on top of me and puts her mouth on my mouth. "Listen to what I say, James. Look into my eyes so you know how true these words are. You brought me back to life, Flannery."

"What's that you say?"

"You crept into my heart."

"What's that?" I says, like I can't hear too good.

"I'm in love with you." She stares at me nose to nose. "Say it, you son of a saint," she says, "or I'll bite your nose off."

"I want you should move in with me," I says. "I got a flat with three rooms and a bath and a half."

"I get the bath and you get the half?"

"Except I'm caught short," I agree.

"What kind of bed?"

"King size."

"I get the right side, you get the left?"

"What is this, a contract negotiation?"

"That comes later," she says. "This is for openers."

"Whatever you want, I agree to," I says.

"Don't," she says, "I don't like *everything* to come so easy."

She brings some of her things to my flat, but not all of her things. She's ready to try, but sleeping in my bed instead of hers don't mean we're handcuffed together yet. She's more wary than I am. I like it. Because if she wasn't I probably would have took back the offer.

The first morning we're sitting at the breakfast table like a married couple, Stanley walks in. He stands there staring at Mary like she's made of sugar.

I get up and check the door. I took the night chain off when I ran down for a pint of milk and the papers, and didn't put it back on, but the Yale is still on the catch. I go back to the kitchen and Stanley's still standing there checking Mary out.

"How do you do that?" I says.

Stanley looks at me.

"How do you walk through locked doors, Stanley?"

He won't cop, but just looks at me like he's telling me that even the third degree cuts no ice with somebody as tough as him.

Mary's looking at him like she thinks he's adorable.

"Stanley, this is my friend, Mary Ellen Dunne."

Mary sticks out her hand.

"How do you do, Stanley?" she says.

'Ho, May'en Dunne," he says. Then he looks at me and says, "Don't kid me, Jimbly, she ain' you fwen, you wucking her."

That evening my old man stops by to tell me about what he found out at the firehouse, and he sees Mary has moved in. For a minute I wonder is he going to get ditsy about us living together without benefit of wedlock. All parts of a man don't grow the same speed with the times.

"You shouldn't wonder and you don't have to ask," I says. "Marriage is not yet an issue."

"Don't be old-fashioned," he says. "This ain't the thirties."

What he's got to tell me about from the firemen is nothing much. The pipe bomb was homemade. It was constructed mostly of heads of kitchen matches packed tight and was set off with a rubber band and some sandpaper. It was supposed to produce more light and noise than damage, but the pipe was old and corroded inside, so it busted all apart like a grenade.

So, I don't know much, but a little. Enough maybe to run a bluff on this Ciccone, who's one of the newest members of Asbach's crusade. I leave Mary and my old man gabbing away like a pair of old hens.

Ciccone lives in the back of a candy store. Somebody's working a pinball machine.

"Isn't that something?" I says when he opens the door and a wall of wet heat hits me. "I ain't heard one of them things for a long time. Everything's lasers and zaps nowadays."

"Is that what you bring me to the door to tell me?" he says.

He's a skinny little guy, with ears like a jug and a head already going bald, though he can't be any older than me. He's in his underwear.

"I won't lie to you," I says. "I come to talk to you about what happened over to the abortion clinic on Sperry."

"So what about it? You a cop?"

"You know what my father used to say when I stood in front of an open door? 'What do you want to do, heat the outside?' he'd say."

"Your father was some comedian," he says.

"My father's still alive," I says. "He's an old friend of Vito Velletri. Ask me to come in."

"I got nothing to do with Vito Velletri," he says, but steps aside and lets me come in.

A young woman, thin as a bone, half-dressed in a slip, is sitting in a sprung overstuffed chair staring at a color television set that costs the rest of the household furniture put together. Her eyes flick at me and then she goes back to the set.

The place ain't big, but it still has the empty feeling of an abandoned warehouse or a railroad-station toilet. The only pictures on the wall is religious: a bleeding heart wrapped in thorns, a Christ hanging on the cross looking ga-ga with pain, another picture of just His face with closed eyes that, when you look at them hard enough, open up and scare you half to death.

It's so hot and wet in the flat they could sell tickets to a steam. I take off my coat and hat.

"You're not staying," Ciccone says.

"That's right," I says, "but I don't want to melt on the rug. Something wrong with the furnace?"

"The damned thing's right behind that wall," he says.

The wall's stained and dripping like it's raining inside.

"It heats the whole goddamned building, but the pipes what deliver it are right behind that wall and the pipes leak," he goes on.

There's a lot of running around overhead. I glance up. The busted chandelier is even swinging a little.

"You got a zoo up there?" I asks.

"Got a whorehouse," the skinny woman says. "That's why it's got to be so much heat. They running around bare-assed all the time." She don't look at me while she delivers this information.

"My wife don't know what she's talking about," Ciccone says. "She thinks she's a comedian, too."

"You buy a lot of matches?" I says.

"What in the hell is that supposed to mean?"

"You know the kind I mean? The kitchen matches with the blue-and-white heads."

"Sure I know the kind you mean. I don't need kitchen matches. What for would I want kitchen matches?"

"To light your stove."

"It's on a pilot."

"So, not to light your stove. What else can you do with kitchen matches?"

"Agnes, you go in the bedroom, you lock the door," he says.

I got to hand it to him. He thinks he's got a crazy on his hands and he's thinking of the wife.

"What about my program?" she asks, whining like a pup.

"What's it matter?"

She gets up and goes into the next room, dragging her feet like a kid and twitching her unappetizing rump at me like it will drive me mad and I will attack her on the threadbare rug right in front of her husband.

"You didn't answer me what I asked you," he says.

"What's that?"

"I asked you was you a cop."

"I'm not a cop."

"So get the hell out of here."

"I'm a concerned citizen."

"So, go vote."

"I'm also a precinct captain over to the Twenty-seventh where the girl was killed." I take out my money clip, separate a twenty, and hand it to him. "What's a couple of questions?"

"Was it match heads what was used in that bomb that blew up the clinic?" he says, taking the twenty.

I looked surprised . . . because I'm surprised.

"You rolling over this easy? You ready to confess to the first stranger that comes along with twenty bucks in his hand?" I says.

"You crazy? I done nothing except go down to Sperry Avenue to see this girl is really going to go through with it."

"With what?"

"Getting rid of a kid. What do you think they was doing down there, having a floating crap game?"

"Oh, I know what they was doing and I know what those people marching outside the place was doing. I know they was dropping dripping red knives on the step. I know they were cutting off cats' heads."

"Don't look at me. I done none of that. All I done . . ."

"You signed up with that bunch, didn't you?"

". . . was do a favor. Hey! What am I going to do? Some redheaded hag with a mole on her chin shoves a membership card under my nose and gives me five bucks should I sign it."

"Why would she give you five bucks for that?"

"How the hell should I know? Maybe the head of the organization was giving out prizes to the one who signed up the most members. You know, how they do in real-estate offices and used-car lots. Salesman of the month."

"So you sign and take the five."

"And I go inside to see is the girl in the waiting room."

"Is she?" I ask, waiting for him to tell me the girl he was eyeballing is the one with the old woman.

But he tells me, "No, I don't see her."

"See who? I mean, what's the name of this girl you're checking up on?"

"Helen Addison. It ain't her real name."

"Who wanted her checked out?" I says.

"The pimp upstairs."

"Why? Does he want to make sure she's having the abortion?"

"He gives me twenty dollars. That ain't enough for me to go looking into his . . . motivation."

A smile clicks on and off, like a bulb. He's used a new word and didn't break his tongue on it.

"Where was the girl?" I says.

"Well, she was inside the other room, wasn't she? Otherwise she wouldn't of got herself blown to hell."

"What did you do when the bomb went off?"

"I got the hell out of there quick, didn't I? What do I got to do for twenty, spend a night talking to cops?"

"You see an old lady?"

"I think. She was sitting with another kid waiting to get—"

"I don't mean that one. I mean another. Probably wearing a white coat or a smock."

"Yeah. I saw her. I walked over to the hallway and saw her go into a room what said 'Operating' on it."

"She see you?"

"She didn't look. I didn't hang around there. The doorknob rattled on another door. I turned around and went back to the waiting room. I took a seat. I was going to wait for this Helen to come out."

"You know what she looked like? You got a picture of her?"

"Oh, no, I see her before. I see her upstairs."

"Sometimes you work for cash, sometimes for trade?"

"Sometimes," he says, and grins. "Good stuff."

I turn to the door.

"Hey," he says, "where you going?"

"Upstairs."

"Don't you think what I told you is worth another twenty?"

"I figure you for a man who doesn't care about rewards when it comes to doing his civic duty."

"How about ten?"

"I'll send you a municipal citation."

"You don't got to go upstairs you want to play. My old lady's waiting for you right behind that door. Fifty bucks."

I take it back. He was not thinking of the wife, only how to use her.

"You stay out of the sand," I says. "You'll get a sore belly."

11

Upstairs, at the end of a long corridor of doors with painted windows on both sides, there's another door all wood with a Judas hole in the middle of it. I knock and the slide clicks back. I see a black marble in the middle of some egg white staring at me. The door opens a crack. A voice speaks to me on the level of my belly button from a face as black as anthracite.

"You can't come in," the voice of a woman pretending to be a man, or vice versa, says.

"If you don't, Jessie, I'll huff and I'll puff and I'll blow your house down."

"Go away, Flannery. You're nothing but trouble," Jessie says.

"That is not what you said when I got your brother out of jail on that breaking-and-entering charge."

"That was then, and now is now."

"You want I should go get Vice and kick this door down, Jessie?"

It takes a minute, then the door is opened. On the other side of it is a three-step ladder and Jessie Acacia, who is very short and round, with a head of frizzy hair, sometimes yellow and sometimes green. At the moment it's half and half.

"You don't got to call Vice," she says. "Stick around. They'll all be by for a treat sooner or later."

"You show me where the man sits and get out of my way, Jessie . . ."

"Now just a second . . ."

". . . or I'll walk right over you."

"You Irish bastard, I'll spit and break your knee-caps."

"I ain't got time to give you a hug," I says, walking by her toward a door in the back of the hall that has a curtain on the window.

"Hurry back," she says. "I got a favor you should do for me."

I walk into the office, which was once a kitchen, just as Bo Addison puts down the phone.

This Bo Addison is wearing four-hundred-dollar snakeskin shoes, a peach velour suit, and a satin shirt with gold nuggets for cuff links. He smells like a field of lilacs.

"You took a bath," I says.

He showed me his teeth, which ain't even as yellow as they was when he was a poor junk sculptor just a few days ago. I think the man is a chameleon, he's changed so much.

"You lied to me, Bo," I says. "You tell me you ain't a pimp while talking like a pimp, which you figure is not what a pimp would do."

"If I was Bo, I wouldn't have lied to you," he says. "I would have told you to fuck off."

I lean over to get a better look. It ain't Bo.

"You got a twin," I says.

"I got a foolish brother," he says.

"So, tell me what I call you."

"Mr. Addison is nice. What can I do for you, Mr. Precinct Captain Flannery?" He grins and points a clean finger with a well-buffed nail at the floor and Ciccone's flat below.

"Your reputation precedes you," he says.

"What was your brother doing over to Badger Street?"

"My grandmother lives there. She won't live anywhere else no matter how hard I try to move her."

"My old man is the same way. It ain't good to take them out of the old places. Who's your grandmother?"

"Hester Bowling."

"I know her."

"She says you do. She names you when I see you talking to my brother from the window. We was doing some heavy work for her."

"Your brother recruit for you?"

"Sometimes I get him in a suit and let him work the Greyhound station or the parks."

"You let him break any of the rookies in?"

He laughs like I give him a funny thought. "Nookie-rookies," he says. "Bo gets what he can get."

"He fell in love with Helen Caplet?"

"I never said he was smart."

"You're smart, though."

"Yes, I'm smart," he says.

"You're a pimp, and pimps are smart, is that right?"

He's not smiling anymore.

"I'm a social director," he says. "I supply companions and entertainment . . ."

"You're a spoiler and a merchant."

". . . for all sorts of functions and affairs and for . . ."

"You're a trader. A peddler . . ."

". . . some of the most important politicians and dignitaries in the city."

". . . but this is your way of making a living, and I'm not here to pass judgment on you."

"Am I suppose to thank you for that?"

"They come here?"

"What?"

"These important people . . . they come here?"

"Sometimes they come here. But this is more like basic-training camp, you know what I mean? Most of the girls in this camp got no polish yet."

"Who comes here?"

"Blow on out of here, Flannery. This ain't even your turf. You're maybe a big dog over to the Twenty-seventh, but you're just a dog turd over here. This is the Twenty-*fifth*. This is Velletri's ground."

"How come a black has got Velletri for a China-man?"

"Hey, come alive, man, this is the age of black power in Chicago. What color is the mayor?"

"There's still Velletri."

"Even guineas like to get their ashes hauled before they go to church."

"So you won't give me names."

"I won't give you *nothing*."

"I'll go over to Badger Street and tell your grand-mother what you do to make her living," I says.

It's like he gets mad and sad at the same time. He jerks his eyes away from mine and stares up at the corner of the room, looking for some demon who could maybe strike me dead.

Every soul has a soft spot. His grandmother was Addison's.

"What was Helen Caplet . . . Addison . . . what-ever she called herself from one day to another, doing over to Sperry Avenue having an abortion?"

"You think whores don't get caught?"

"I don't think whores get caught as much today as maybe they used to. But I do think whores get senti-mental sometimes, and hungry for a husband or a baby. I think they start dreaming the wrong dreams with the wrong customer. Maybe the John goes along with the lovey-dovey. Why not? It makes the loving sweeter. Maybe he's the dreamer. Maybe because they talk about the future, the whore don't charge a price anymore and that makes the customer feel like a big man."

A laugh rolls up out of Addison's chest. Didn't he know what fools men could make of themselves when it came to women? Even women they'd want no part of outside of bed?

"Ah, you know, sure you do," I says. "Half the

men in Chicago dream about being a pimp, being a
devil with women, having a stable, having a dozen
women roll over for them at the snap of a finger."

"Hell, they couldn't take the heat," Addison says.
"They couldn't do the necessary."

"Or maybe it was your brother gave her the baby
and you didn't want a good soldier taken out of the
line. And didn't want your brother's head scrambled
by a honky whore."

"If it was that way, I would've give her to him.
What the hell do I care? This world makes whores
faster than you and me can use them up."

"But it don't make brothers."

"Bo lives his own life. I don't fret about it."

"So, who was the con who conned the con, the
whoremonger who turned the whore? Who was this
Helen and who was her mark?"

"I don't know."

"Ah, don't *you* be a fool."

"I truly do not know."

"Am I supposed to believe that?"

"Helen wasn't in my string. She was independent.
She came and went as she pleased. I just give her a
place to do her thing. I contract her some customers
when there's more action than my regular girls can
take."

"Why would you waste your time on a woman you
don't own?"

"Every fish don't take the bait the same," Addison
says. "A good fisherman, he's patient. There would
come a time . . ."

There always comes a time.

". . . when she would want a favor. Want a thousand for a coat. Want a couple lines of coke. I know
how to wait. I ain't a rough man with these women,
Flannery."

"She was somebody's favorite."

"That could be. That could very well be."

"She give you a number where you could reach her when you needed her for an extra?"

"She does me the courtesy of calling in every morning when she's willing to work."

"You slipped Ciccone a twenty . . ."

"A tenner."

". . . to see that Helen really did have an abortion?"

"I do the favor for a man who calls me on the phone."

"A customer?"

"I don't know the voice."

"But it could have been a customer of yours?"

"Sure, and it could have been one of the special reserve Helen keeps for herself."

"So why do you do a blind favor that costs you even a ten?"

"Because he sends over a hundred by messenger. I'm a businessman."

"Is that all you're going to give me?"

"That's all I got."

I don't think so. I think he's been told to clam up. I caught him just hanging up the phone. I figure, since it only takes a minute for Ciccone to tip him off about me, I caught Addison checking in with somebody else. Otherwise he could have given me what he knew about a dead whore and he would have had my marker for some day.

I have the feeling that somebody might be quick enough to be waiting for me downstairs. When nobody's waiting for me, I relax so quick it gives me a pain in the back.

12

My old man is gone home by the time I get back to my flat. The place already looks and smells different. I'm reminded of something my father told me long ago. "Women are powerful," he said. "They'll change the world."

I see, now, he means *my* world.

"You've been a long time," Mary said. "Did you get what you went after?"

"You shouldn't have waited up," I says.

She takes my coat and hat. She sits me down in the big chair. She sits on the floor and takes off my shoes.

"Listen to me, James," she says. "I won't interfere in what you do. I won't complain about how late you have to stay out to do it sometimes. I won't even insist you tell me anything you think I shouldn't know. Those are things you have all the say about. But I'll do what I do. And one of the things I'll do is wait up for you as long as we're under the same roof together. If I'm living alone, I'll sleep alone, but if I'm living with you, I won't sleep alone. Not ever. Not if I can help it."

"I've got to get used to it," I says. "I been coming home to an empty house—not even a cat—for eight years."

"Do you want something to eat?"

I realize, with some surprise, that I'm hungry. She knows that too. Pretty soon she'll be throwing me over her shoulder and burping me. I don't mind.

She makes me some scramble and ham. While I'm eating I tell her everything I done. It feels so good to have someone to talk to.

The phone rings.

"Two o'clock in the morning," Mary says.

"It can't be good news," I says.

When I lift up the receiver, at first I think I got a breather. Then a voice says, "Check it out. There was a bullet in Helen Caplet."

Down at the morgue I got a friend I go to school with when we was in grammar school.

When we're thirteen and fourteen Eddie Fergusen and Dick Hodgson and me run around after school. We play softball and toss baskets and squeeze Sheila Coletti's big tits on the school steps after the sun goes down in the summer. We're the Three Musketeers and buy us jackets which is all the same—black with red braiding—but we ain't a gang like the gangs that made trouble.

Except once we decide to steal.

Mr. Fidel owns the candy store on the corner in the neighborhood where we play pinball and drink cherry phosphates. He's a grouch with a quick temper. He tosses somebody out and bans them forever and ever, about five times a week. He would've had no customers younger than twenty, except nobody believes him and are back the next day. The only one he really likes is Eddie, because Eddie is the sweetest con you'd ever meet, even at fourteen.

Fidel has this kid, Ernie Kepler, who's clever with his hands, fixing clocks and watches and things like toasters. He's got him in the back room doing repairs and taking 50 percent: that's exploitation. He's not declaring his earnings to the federal government: that's fraud. He's stashing the undeclared cash in the ice-cream freezer: that's tempting.

We figure we got a case against him and he should

be taught a lesson, not to exploit Ernie Kepler and not to defraud the government. So, one week in summer, we make up this plan to break and enter through the window in the alley to the back room, then through the connecting door to the candy store, to which Eddie says he's got a key which works.

Eddie tells us this, just like he tells us he'll leave his softball and mitt in the back room for some reason, and come back for it just at the minute Fidel is going to lock the front door. Then he'll open the catch on the alley window so we don't got to break it.

After supper, I tell my father and mother I'm going out to play a game of kick the can with the guys. I get Dick and we go to get Eddie, who lives on the second floor of a house with a porch. He comes out in his pajamas and says his aunt, who he lives with, won't let him come out because he forgot to do something for her which she told him to do. Here is this thief can't come out because his aunt won't let him.

It's ridiculous and we should've quit right there, but Eddie throws down the key to the store and tells us to go do it without him. Now he has put Dick and me on our nerve. We chicken out and he'll never let us forget. That's how dumb Dick and me are.

We go down to the alley and Dick goes through the window that Eddie has opened just the way it was planned. I squat down in the dark alley with a hunting knife, which I don't know what the hell I expect to do with should anybody see me. Dick sticks his head out the window and tells me the key, which Eddie said would open the door, won't. He takes a hammer and screwdriver from Ernie Kepler's workbench and tries to tap the dried paint off the hinges so we can take the door off.

While I'm crouching there with the knife sweating in my hand and my heart beating so loud I can hardly hear the tapping Dick is making, the kitchen door to the downstairs flat opens up and Mrs. Fidel, who's hard-of-hearing but has good eyes, puts out the empties for the milk man. I'm dying should she look up and see me. She doesn't and goes back inside.

I stick my head through the back window and tell Dick the hell with it. He grabs a carton of cigarettes and a big box of hard candy. We go down to the freight yards to divvy it out. The cigarettes is all right, but the candy is stale old penny candy that tastes like soap.

It's the last time Dick and me ever try to do anything like that. But Eddie, who, maybe because he didn't have the scare I had, tries it on his own another time. He robs an auto supply and gets away with it. Pretty soon he steals so many times without getting caught, he thinks his life is charmed.

Then he gets caught and tried and sentenced. By this time I got some influence. I give out plenty of markers and call in plenty more. It busts my accounts all over town, but I get him on a work release program and quick probation. I get him a job in the morgue, which he likes.

I got his marker for life.

He's as cheery as ever when he comes out of the locker room wearing his white coat. "What can I do you?" Eddie says.

"You got a dead girl in a drawer."

"I got lots."

"This is the one that got blown up over to Sperry Avenue."

"That one was so young and good-looking it's a shame," he says.

I don't ask him if it ain't a shame should somebody young and ugly or old and used up gets blown away.

"Can I see?" I says.

"Whatever you want. Follow me."

We go into the room with all the brushed steel

drawers stacked along one wall. He goes to one of
them and pulls it out. She's under a green sheet. He
strips it almost all the way down to her ankles. She's
been autopsied and that ain't very pretty . . .

"Jesus, Mary and Joseph."

. . . but they have put her back together so at least
her face looks . . . maybe not like she's sleeping, but
maybe not so bad.

Her face is hard, though, with them tight little
lines like razor cuts around her mouth. Like women
get who've been used too much, too soon. Even
dead, she looks like she's frowning, warning the world
that she'll fight if it ain't careful.

"Can I read the medical examiner's report?"

"No, you can't."

"Hey, Eddie," I says.

For such a small matter I don't want to remind
him of the debt he owes me. That ain't how it's done.

"I would if I could, but I can't," he says. "It walked
away."

"Lost?"

"Strayed or stolen," he says. "I'd bet on stolen."

"You read her report?" I asks.

"I read them all," Eddie says, grinning, having had
his tease at my expense. "I got time on my hands."

"What killed her?"

"What do you think?"

"A bullet."

Eddie points to the little round hole in the middle
of a bruise, right under her left breast, toward the
center of the chest.

"Where's the bullet?" I asks.

"Gone with the wind, the same like the report.
How did you figure it was gunshot? It ain't in the
papers."

"A little bird told me," I says.

"The little bird got a name?"

"For a minute I thought it was you, Eddie."

He shakes his head. "It would've been if I knew you was interested," he says. "But how would I know?"

"Cover her up," I says.

Eddie pulls up the sheet and covers her body up to the neck. For a minute she looks peaceful like Mrs. Klutzman looked, then Eddie pulls the sheet up over her face.

13

I go down to the clinic on Sperry. The Right-to-Lifers are still marching outside, but there's only three of them. The redheaded lady with the mole is one. She hurries over to me and shoves a membership blank under my nose.

"Five dollars to join a holy crusade."

"A couple days ago you *gave* a friend of mine five dollars to join."

"Did I?"

"Why did you do that?"

"Because I got ten dollars for every new crusader I signed up."

"How's that?"

"Mr. Asbach needed names to make a case with some heavy contributors."

"He doesn't need them anymore?"

"We hit the news," she says, as though stunned at my lack of sophistication about media matters.

"So now I got to pay to get in?" I says.

"You want to get in?"

"If I join, where does my five dollars go?"

"For printing circulars. For making signs."

"For making bombs?" I says.

"I know you," she says. "You threatened Mr. Asbach . . . the man is a saint. You lied to me. You told me you was one of us."

"We're all one in the Lord," I says.

"Are you a Christian?"

"You're damned right," I says.

"You ain't a Catholic?"

"Catholics ain't Christian?"

"Is the Pope a Polack?"

"Can we talk?"

"About what?"

"About maybe I should take out a membership, maybe four or five."

She swivels her head around and pops her eyes to see if the other marchers have heard me mention such riches.

"Over here," she says, and scuttles over to the telephone pole with her sign dragging behind her like it was a busted rudder.

"Tell me the truth," she says, "you really don't want to join this bunch, do you?"

"Tell me the truth," I says, "you really don't give a damn, do you? This is a living for you, ain't it?"

"A supplement to my income, which ain't much," she says.

"Who else do you march for?"

"Anyone who lets me solicit memberships."

"How do you split?"

"Fifty-fifty sometimes. Sometimes I pay a flat and take what I take. It depends."

"Like sometimes you even pay half of what the organizer pays you for a member like you did the other day?"

"Only when it's slow. You're such a fast learner I should maybe make you a partner," she says sarcastically.

"So what's the new arrangement you got with Asbach now that he don't need to pay for numbers?"

"Fifty-fifty."

"Fifty-fifty of five is lunch money. Fifty-fifty of twenty or twenty-five is an abuse to your good nature."

"You see it that way, too?"

"I do. Who wants to be a joiner anyway? I pay you four memberships. You keep the memberships."

"Make it five memberships."

I hand her two tens and a five.

"What can I do you?"

"This Asbach—"

"The man is a saint. Hey." She grins like a child. "You started my tape."

"You got a hell of an act," I says. "This Asbach . . . where was he when the bomb went off?"

"Not here. That what you want to know? Not here, but he was here *before* the bomb went off."

"How long before?"

"Half an hour. Make it forty-five minutes. I count while I march. He stopped by to tell us to fight the good fight. The two-faced sonofabitch."

"Two-faced? How two-faced?"

"Here he's got us stomping around pestering poor women who got caught and want to get rid of a burden. It ain't easy for most of them. It hurts them in the heart. You can tell. You can see it in their eyes."

"Two-faced?" I says, reminding her.

"He's shouting and screaming about what these poor girls done and how they got caught because they was too lazy . . ."

She maybe means innocent or trusting, but there's no way for her to say a soft thing like that, because she's afraid she'll get laughed at.

". . . and he's got a tart in the back of the cab. He's off to lay on his back while we got to stand on our feet."

"Did Asbach go inside the clinic?"

"No."

"Did Asbach talk to anyone except you people on the street?"

"No."

"Look," I says. "You take maybe a quarter pound of Epsom salts, your feet ache, and put it in a pan of hot water with some thyme and sage like you use for stuffing. Let me tell you, it'll do wonders."

"I'll try it," she says, and her hand comes out with my bills in it, like she's touched by my concern for her feet and is even thinking about giving me back my twenty-five. Before she can catch herself doing a dumb thing, I close my hand around her fingers and smile at her.

"And maybe buy yourself a pair of sheepskin slippers."

"Hey," she says, "you're all right."

"Vote Democrat," I says.

What the hell, a vote for the party is a vote for the party, even if I don't know if she lives in my precinct.

I go inside.

Chapman is stripped to his skivvy shirt. He's got arms like pipe stems wrapped in thongs. While I watch, he picks up a sheet of wallboard like it was made of tissue paper and lays it against the studs of a partition. A small woman, who's wearing a tool belt, starts swinging a hammer and nailing the panel like she knows what she's doing. She does a long row like she's tapping out a tune.

He turns around, taking a step and reaching for the next piece of board like he's a dancer. He pauses when he sees me. "Is there something else?" he says.

The woman eyes me up and down. She has a pretty face like a moon with pink spots of color on her cheeks.

"This is my wife, Gloria," Chapman says.

I put out my hand. "I'm Jim Flannery," I says.

She pulls off her work glove and sticks out her hand, which is warm and dry and solid as a stone. She takes off the bandanna that covers her hair and shakes her head. Masses of black curls come tumbling down around her face.

"Thank you," Chapman says.

"For what?"

"For not acting surprised. For not wincing."

"I ain't going to like you," I says, "you keep on acting grateful."

"It's that or be mad all the time," Gloria says. "Cal can't make up his mind."

"I got the same trouble and I ain't black," I says.

"So, what can I do for you?" Chapman says.

"I want you should identify somebody for me."

"Who?"

"The guy who you saw entering the waiting room as you passed through the hall on your way to your office."

"Is he in custody?"

"What for? I know where he lives. I just want you to look."

"Right now?"

"No, it can wait for a little. How about tonight? How about you and your wife come over to my place and have supper with me and my friend? We can go over to the Twenty-fifth, where this guy lives, after we eat."

Chapman hesitates, like he's not particularly anxious to get social with me.

"Mary Ellen Dunne is my friend," I says, "and we can leave the ladies to talk while we go have a look."

Chapman smiles. It's nice and open and friendly. "Hey, don't tell me," he says. "You mean to say you're going out with Mary Ellen Dunne?"

"In a manner of speaking," I says. "That knock you down?"

"Well, no, but it's like getting a seal of approval stamped on your forehead, so far as I'm concerned, if Mary Ellen Dunne trusts you. She reads people's hearts."

"What time?" Gloria says.

I look at my watch. "Six?" I says.

"That's all right."

I take off my coat and hat and put them on a chair. Chapman watches me as though he's amused and startled. I roll up my sleeves.

"That's a good suit," Gloria says.

"You sure you want to do this?" Chapman says. "It's hard work for a man who isn't used to it."

"You're a doctor. You used to it?"

"I've done more than my share."

"What do you think, I was born with a cigar in my mouth, a derby on my head, a ten-dollar payoff in one hand and a ballot in the other?"

When I tell Mary that Chapman and his wife is coming for supper, she smiles and asks me what I told them about us.

"Nothing."

"Are we hiding?" she asks.

"No. I just don't think who we tell, except for my father, that we're living together, is only up to me. You got a say."

"Well, say it or don't say it, Gloria will know even if Dr. Chapman doesn't."

"Doctor? Is that what you're going to call him? Is that what I'm supposed to call him?"

"Professional courtesy," Mary says. "It's a habit."

"I know."

"I suppose, since it's social, we'll call him Calvin."

"You call him Calvin, I'll call him Cal," I says.

They arrive right on the dot. Gloria's got a little bunch of flowers. Chapman's got a bottle of wine in a paper sack. Everybody is happy, also shy.

Gloria is happy because when a white woman marries a black man she's going to see more black faces than white all the time.

Chapman is happy because he hopes maybe the

world ain't always going to be black and white like it was when his mother works scrubbing floors day and night to get him through school. Maybe our generation, and the ones coming right after, will be color-blind.

Mary is happy because she's got a secret she wants the world to know and these people will be kind messengers.

I'm happy because it's like we've been married some time, and here we are having a couple over for supper, and the flat looks better then I remember it ever looking.

"So, let's eat," I says. "You like Irish stew?"

"Hungarian goulash," Mary says.

When he finishes his second plate, Chapman says, "That is the best hotpot I've tasted in a long time."

That, I guess, is how different people make friends.

Mary won't stay behind when I say Chapman and me is going over to the Twenty-fifth so Chapman can have a look at Ciccone.

We can't leave Gloria behind all on her own, so we all go down to the Twenty-fifth together in Chapman's car, which has got more room than mine. It takes guts to do what he's doing. It's all right a black should maybe drive through this part of the Twenty-fifth, but to get out and walk even from the curb to a door ain't such a good idea. If anything, having a black mayor makes it worse for the blacks in certain wards and parts of wards. Addison, the pimp, is a special case. He's useful.

Somebody's playing the pinball machine in the candy store. Upstairs a woman laughs like a parrot. I knock on the door of Ciccone's flat.

The door opens up, and the smell and heat like wet wash hits me in the face again. Ciccone stands there in his underwear.

"Why do you bother me?" he says. "Am I a freak? You selling tickets for people should look at me? Why do you bring a nigger to my house?"

"You work for any black man who pays you a tenner."

"It was twenty," Ciccone says.

"It was ten, so don't get smart," I says.

"That's the man in the waiting room," Chapman says.

"That *isn't* the man I saw in the corridor," Mary says.

"You've got a bad mouth," Gloria says.

Ciccone slams the door in my face.

We start back to the car.

"Wait a minute," I says. "I got a question I got to ask from somebody upstairs. You wait in the car." I look at Chapman. "I mean wait *in* the car."

Upstairs, Jessie's eye is at the Judas hole the minute I knock. This time she opens the door right away.

"I didn't get to ask you the favor," she says.

"So ask me," I says.

"I forget what it was, but I'll think about it."

"Jessie, you pick gum wrappers off the street. You collect string. You can't let a bargain pass you by. You think I owe you a favor because you open a door even when you got no favor to ask. I give you my marker. You can call it in any time inside of a month."

"You keep poking and nosing, you won't live that long," Jessie says.

"Will you mourn for me?" I says.

"I'll pee on your grave," she says.

I go down the hall and open the door to Addison's office without knocking. He's grinning at a white whore who's sitting on his lap. His hand is on her tit.

"Don't do that," I says, "I got to ask you a question."

"Didn't Velletri give you the word?"

"Did you call him the other night?"

He don't say nothing, but stands up so the whore has to scramble to stay on her feet. She goes away without him having to say go away.

"Are you going to call him again?" I says.

"I got orders," he says.

"What game are you playing?"

"What do you mean?"

"You sent your brother down to give me Helen Caplet's name."

"If you think that, what does it tell you?" he says.

"That maybe it's you who fell for a whore."

"You're a joke, Flannery."

"So what about the other thing you tell me?"

"What other thing?"

"The bullet in Helen Caplet's chest."

"Oh, my," he says, and he flashes me his white, white smile. "You're just trying that on. I don't tell you nothing."

"I got an ear like a musician. I play the harmonica. I read your name in your whispers, but it only just come to me when I'm standing downstairs. It was you on the phone."

He stands up, bored with me and my tricks. "Hey," he says, waving his pink palm in my face, "take what you think you got."

"One more question?"

"I got no more answers."

"Favor for favor. You answer my question, I don't tell Velletri you talk out of both sides of your mouth."

He stares at me like I'm dirt he intends to some-day wipe off his shoe. "You ought to clean the wax out of your ears. I don't tell you about no bullet in Helen because I don't know about no bullet in Helen."

"There's a guy named Joe Asbach . . ."

"Yeah, he's a customer. He comes around."

"Is he more than a customer?"

Addison has the trick of lifting his eyebrows, too.

"Do you give customers the right to take your women out on approval?" I says.

"They got their own lives. Ain't you heard? White slavery went out in the thirties."

"Who was the woman was with him the day of the bombing?"

"Mavis Concord. The one you just saw on my lap."

I turn my head like I'm hoping she's standing in the corner waiting for me to talk to her.

"She's gone, Flannery, she's long gone."

Back at the flat we have coffee and cake. Gloria and Mary act like they're already sisters. Chapman and me aren't brothers, but whatever there is to like about another man seems to make the atmosphere good in the kitchen.

Every once in a while Gloria's hand comes over to Chapman's and she touches him like she wants him to know she's there. Mary touches mine, too, like it's the same.

I look at Chapman's black face and Gloria's sweet white face and I wonder what the crap is all about. People ain't got enough reasons to kill each other they got to do it for color or language or the way they face God?

My old man comes barging in just when they're leaving. He shakes Chapman's hand and looks him in the eye, and charms Gloria out of her shoes.

When the door is closed behind them and Mary is out in the kitchen piling the dishes in the sink, he says, "What are you doing with a nigger in the house?"

I look at him for a minute like I don't even know him. "Why do you want to say something like that for?"

"Let me tell you, when I went to fires down to the nigger wards or was sent down in the summer to turn off the hydrants which they turned on . . ."

". . . to get some relief from the goddamned heat . . ."

". . . so they should get cool," my father finishes, and looks down his nose at me, "which they got a perfect right to do. My supervisor at the time, Willy Hanrahan, who is dead these twenty years—God rest his soul—warns me not to cut myself because them people has got all kinds of venereal disease which can kill me."

"Oh, for Christ's sake," I says, when somebody says something like that to you with a straight face, so you know they mean it, what else can you say?

"Don't take His name in vain," my old man says.

"I'm calling on Him to save the bigots," I says. "Besides, you come on about how you don't like the blacks and who's your best friend over to the fire-house for forty years? Amos Washington, the janitor, is who. And who's the man you spend hours talking with when he's pushing his barrow and collecting junk? Whistlin' Sam is who."

"Well, they was different—God keep them both— you know? Amos was the best Christian I ever knew and Sam put three children through college collecting trash in a cart. Not a truck. Not a horse and wagon. With a goddamned pushcart, and he had the arthritis so bad he'd sometimes weep right in front of me."

"Three children through college?" I says.

"One a lawyer, one a college professor, and one a doctor."

"Well. Calvin's a doctor," I says.

"There you go," my old man says, as if that made *his* case. But what his case was I'd forgotten long before.

"You know this fireman, Warnowski?" he says, making up to me and giving me no time to think about how he picked my pocket of my argument.

"I'm talking to your leader, Delvin, this morning. He tells me how you made such a beautiful case for this public servant, who drives his car into the river and kills himself while rushing to answer an alarm because he cuts the wheel to avoid a kiddy who runs in front of him, that he passes it on to the commissioner. They're not only going to give Warnowski's widow full-pension benefits, but they're writing up a commendation for Warnowski which the mayor is going to sign, and there's talk of putting Warnowski up for fireman of the year."

14

Mary's already gone to work at the hospital by the time I get up. A big black sedan is waiting in front of Pakula's grocery store. Two panthers named Ginger and Finks, one with a pencil mustache, the other without, are lounging on the fenders, front and back. I don't even wait for the invitation. I open the door to the back seat myself and get in.

"You're fast on your feet, Jimmy," Finks says.

"Did I give you permission to call me by my first name?" I says.

"Mr. Flannery," he says, "you got more balls than brains."

Vito Velletri, the warlord of the Twenty-fifth, works out of an office that looks like the office of an insurance-company president. It's all polished wood, thick carpets, and brass lamps. The curtains at the windows, which block an ugly view, are made of dark-red velvet.

Velletri himself looks like a Vatican monsignor, small, neat, with a nun's quiet hands and a cardinal's natural air of power. He's born in Sicily sixty years ago, so his accent is smooth at the edges except when he's mad and then he sounds like he's just off the boat. Velletri don't raise his voice above a whisper. Even the mob don't dare to mess him around very much. He's a diplomat. He's a good father to his people.

Velletri's not a criminal, even though he's accused

every election year of favoring the mob. He promised to deliver the Twenty-fifth to Richard Daley, Jr., in the '83 primary, but it goes to the black candidate. Maybe for the first time he wakes up to the facts of life. The blacks, who've been patient and quiet all these years while white men gave jobs to white men in black wards, have been patiently and quietly making babies and taking over blocks with black immigrants from other parts of Chicago and other states. The Twenty-fifth is black, and he finally knows it. That's why Addison. Velletri is making accommodations, though the word is out that he's unhappy. The machine is getting rusty, wearing out, and maybe it's time to get out of the driver's seat before it busts to pieces under him and lands him in the mud.

But power's a hard drug to kick. The hardest. He still wants to use it while he's got it in his hands. He wants to do favors. He wants to make people owe him even though he'll probably never have reason to ask for his payoff—not with a vote and not with a favor. He likes having Lenten breakfasts with the cardinal and spaghetti dinners with the mob bosses.

Of course he's got mob connections. Everybody in Chicago politics has got mob connections. Just about everybody in Chicago society has got mob connections. Who would *not* have mob connections if they're in the money or in the public eye?

"Why you coming into my ward without asking my permission, Mr. Flannery?" he says.

I don't like he should call me Mr. Flannery. My old man knows Velletri a long time. I know Velletri since I'm twenty. Maybe we don't sit down to a private meal together, but we've shared bread and salt at weddings, christenings, and fund-raisers. He should treat me more personal and he's not, so I know that whatever he's about to tell me is serious. Outside the club.

"Mr. Velletri, a thing happened in my district which a person from this district was involved in."

"Mr. Ciccone?"

"Yes, Ciccone, and a pimp that operates upstairs from Ciccone."

"Mr. Addison?"

"Yes, Addison, and a girl who turned a few tricks in his establishment from time to time."

"Miss Caplet?"

"Yes, that girl who was blown up over to Sperry Avenue."

"She was the victim," Velletri says. "That's not involved like we mean involved."

"She's *more* than involved like we mean involved. She's blown up."

"This Joe Asbach is a fanatic."

"The police release him with no warning. He tells me to whistle like he's the cock of the walk."

"So the police are giving him rope, that's all."

I give him a shrug. What the hell am I supposed to say to that? Am I to agree with his notion that the police are so clever, so crafty? Am I to say I've been to the morgue and saw the bullet hole in Helen Caplet? Am I to say there ain't no bullet and no autopsy report anymore, and if someone don't keep an eye out, there may not be a Helen Caplet either; that she maybe could get lost, strayed, or stolen, too? Am I to say that someone murdered this girl because she was involved one hell of a lot more than we mean involved?

"There's no evidence that this Helen Caplet, if this is her name, lived in my ward," Velletri says.

"She worked in your ward from time to time, Mr. Velletri," I says. "I got no other place to start looking for this dead girl's people except here in the Twenty-fifth."

"I understand that," he says agreeably. "What I

don't understand is why you're bothering yourself with a whore who wasn't one of your people."

"She dies—is murdered—in my precinct."

"Yes, the honor of your house. I understand that, too. But what do you expect to do about her? Are you a vigilante out to avenge this death? If you are, the revenge doesn't belong to you. It properly belongs to her family. If not to her family, to the law. If not to the law, to me."

"I'm not looking for revenge," I says. "That's the way feuds begin. I understand favor for favor, but not blood for blood. No, Mr. Velletri, I don't even look for revenge for the old woman who *was* one of mine and never did no harm. She's an innocent bystander and I'm sorry she's gone, but it's not the dream of my life to bring her killer down. I'd like to see someone called on these killings, because I don't want people thinking they can walk into my precinct and do whatever they want. Besides—"

"Are we back to Helen Caplet?"

"I'd like to find her family. If she ain't got a family and if nobody comes forward, I don't want she should be buried in the county field. I'll claim her and see she's buried with rites and a stone to mark the grave."

"That's generous," Velletri says, "but you leave that to me. You've made a case for this girl. Until—if—we find out she lived somewhere else, I say she lived in this ward. The Twenty-fifth will do what's right. So, that settles all your reasons for making trips into my ward. Not that you won't be welcome otherwise."

That means I'm supposed to go.

I'm at the door when he says, "Jimmy, do I have your word that you'll leave this matter to me?"

I'm thinking that I'm not so sure. He's put me on notice about stirring anything up in the Twenty-fifth. He's got that right, it's his back yard, but somebody did murder in my precinct and I'm still not so sure I can just turn my back on that.

"Let me think about that, Mr. Velletri," I says.

Velletri nods his head very slowly at me, like he's blessing me, or like he's deciding which of my legs to break.

That evening, I tell Mary what happened.

"So, are you?" she says.

"Am I what?"

"Going to do what Velletri asks?"

She reads my silence like a page.

"Aren't you satisfied you've done everything you can?" she says.

"What do you think?"

"What do I think? I think that you've done everything you could have done. Helen Caplet will be on a missing-persons flyer or she won't. Either way, someone else has the responsibility."

"There's Mrs. Klutzman."

"She's under the ground. You'll tell me stories about her from time to time. I know that you will because the people in the district are your family, your children. That's the best you can do for her."

"Is it right the people who set the bomb should get off without a word?"

"No, it's not right. It's not right those people should do violence when all the time they're saying they want to stop violence being done to unborn children. Are they bad people? I don't know. They're wrong, I think, but I don't know if they're bad. If they set a bomb and it went off at the wrong time when there were still people in the clinic, a judge and jury might even wonder what kind of punishment they should offer. Maybe I'd wonder, too."

I don't tell her the device used to set off the bomb was just an unwinding rubber band, nothing so precise as a clockwork set for an hour when the clinic would be empty. The bomb was set to cover the bullet. A stupid man's notion. The bomber took no care and an old woman who wanted to help a little got killed. Mary could of got killed, too.

"You're not a cop," Mary says.

"You're right," I says.

I look for Pescaro and run him down in a deli over on Powell. He's having a pastrami with warm pickles which they heat for him in the steamer. I never heard of a person, except for Pescaro, ever doing such a thing. It's a very human thing for him to do.

"Can I sit?" I says.

"Sure you can sit," he says. "You can even eat if you want, as long as I don't have to pay."

"Why did you let Joe Asbach go?"

"Because we got nothing on him. Not a thing. He's got eyewitnesses he's elsewhere. He's got a lady . . ."

"A whore."

". . . a professional lady who swears she was with him. This professional lady has other friends that swear by her honesty. They say she'll do things like a monkey and swing by her tail, but she won't tell a lie."

"Who are these friends?"

"You couldn't get that out of me, even with a subpoena," he says. "Be smart. What evidence you think you can find that will pin a match bomb to this Asbach . . ."

"Maybe his people . . ."

". . . or one of his people?"

". . . could be brought in and questioned."

"We got nothing, I tell you. Let it go at that. That's all the conversation I got for you if it's the only subject you know."

"Hey, you should forgive me," I says. "Like the cat, the Irish got curiosity. I didn't look you up to ask questions. Velletri talked to me. He said he'd make my concern for the killings his concern. He said he'd see the right thing done." I'm watching

Pescaro like a bird with a worm. He doesn't flinch. "I got no interest anymore."

"So, why did you run me down while I'm eating, then?"

"To thank you for the favor."

"I done you a favor?"

"When I brought you the knife, you took special interest with the clinic on Sperry."

"I told a car to roll by now and then."

"I mean the man inside the clinic."

"I didn't put no man inside."

"He had a badge."

"Give me a sawbuck, I'll buy you a badge any costume shop," Pescaro says. "You want a pickle?"

I make a face.

"What kind of badge?" he says.

I just look at him.

"Hey, private detective," he says, "it could have been a deputy sheriff's badge. It could have been a Mickey Mouse badge."

When I get back to the flat, Mary is making supper.

"I been eating in restaurants or out of a can for so long I don't know if my stomach will take home cooking," I said.

"It'll take this," she says. "I'm going to make you healthy."

I go up behind her and put my arms around her and stick my nose in her neck. "I think I'll eat you for supper," I says.

"I'm a late-night snack," she says.

"Answer me a question?"

"Sure."

"I don't want you to think about it. I just want you to make a picture in your head and blurt out what you see."

"Go ahead."

"You're in the corridor and this guy who says he's a cop flashes his badge."

"That's right."

"What kind of badge?"

"Sheriff's office," she says straight out, and then looks as though she's surprised herself.

"Was the badge in anything?"

"A leather folder like people wear for identification. You know, the kind that folds over so you can slip it into your top pocket with the ID hanging out."

"What was the badge number?"

"Two . . . No, the two was in the middle."

"Of how many numbers?"

"Something two something. Three numbers, I think."

I give her a squeeze.

"Hey, let me think. Maybe I can do better."

"I don't think so. The way this thing works is, it works the first time or it don't work at all."

"What's it all about?"

"I thought the guy you talked to in the corridor was a city cop sent by the captain. He wasn't."

"He was impersonating?"

"I don't think so. Pescaro mentioned he could buy a badge for ten bucks, but I think whoever the guy was just used what he already had on him when you bumped into him."

After supper Mary says she's going over to her flat in Benjamin Alley and get some more of her things.

"Why don't we get everything?" I says.

"Where would we put it?"

"Some of your furniture could go in storage. The rest could come here. Why waste the rent?"

"Hold it," she says. "Slow down. We're still just trying this on. And don't bother about the rent. A new nurse at the hospital needed a place. I gave her a sublet until we see . . ."

"I'll come with you," I says.

"What for? I could be hours picking up this and that."

"Who's going to carry anything heavy?"

"I'm not a titmouse . . ."

"A what?"

". . . and Joan isn't a bird either."

"No, I'm coming with you," I says. "I don't want you going around alone at night."

"I've been alone for some time."

"You ain't anymore."

There's a knock on the door while Mary's getting her coat and I'm getting mine. I open up and Pakula stands there with some forms in his hand.

"I'm sorry to bother," he says, glancing at Mary, but asking no questions and making no comments, not even hello—like she's not even there unless I say so—"but I get these forms from some county tax man. I don't know what they mean or what I'm expected to do. Could you help me?"

Mary says, "He'll help you . . ."

"Joseph Pakula."

". . . Mr. Pakula."

"He owns the grocery downstairs," I says.

"My name is Mary Ellen Dunne, and I suppose I'll see you when I come down to shop."

"Joe, I don't think . . ." I start to say.

"James will be happy to help you," Mary says. "That's what he does best."

She kisses me and Pakula blushes, and she's gone out the door like a breeze.

"Such a woman," Pakula says with great admiration.

The forms is the usual mess, asking more than is needed, filling up pages so it shouldn't be easy to make a living. It isn't ten minutes the phone rings. I feel a freeze on the back of my hands and the back of my neck. Irish ghosts are dancing across a grave.

Mary's voice is pulled tight like a wire.

"Come to my place, James. Come right away," she says.

"What is it, Mary?" I says, with my heart in my throat.

"I'm not hurt. I'm safe. There's nothing to tell you that you won't see for yourself. Please, please come as soon as you can."

15

I got a portable red flasher with a magnetic base
which I put on the roof when I want to drive like I
usually don't drive. I got a siren under the hood
which I don't use except maybe three times a year. I
get to Mary's flat in three minutes and run up the
stairs. The door is off the latch and open a crack.
I'm ready to give her hell, I'm so scared. She shouldn't
leave the door off the latch no matter what's inside.
There's more than one crazy running around.

I push open the door. A woman is laying on the
floor in the middle of the throw rug. She's got hair
almost the color of Mary's and is built similar. She's
wearing a white nurse's uniform which is red with
blood all over the front. Her head is turned away
from me, and one arm is thrown up with the hand
curled the way a baby's hand curls when it's asleep.

Mary's sitting sideways on the daybed with her legs
pulled up under her. She's hugging herself and staring out the window. She don't blink.

"Mary," I says.

She looks at me and for a second I never see
anybody so scared. Then her face crumples up like a
wet paper towel and the tears start coming down her
cheeks like twin rivers.

I make a circle around the dead woman and take
Mary in my arms. I feel such a rage in me for
whoever done this thing that I feel like a big balloon
in my chest is ready to bust and my eyelids is on fire.

She cries out like an Arab, high wails like a dog or

a human in terrible pain. It rises and falls like sirens going by. People from the other flats start gathering in the doorway, dressed like people are dressed when home in the evening, some in sweaters, some in shirt sleeves, some in their bathrobes. Why do I even register all that while my woman is screaming her heart out?

I catch the eye of a tall man with the face of an undertaker, long like a hound or a horse.

"Use the phone in your flat and get the police over here," I says.

He nods and turns away. All the rest just stand there staring. Mary stops wailing and settles into a moan for a very short time, then stops altogether.

"Why did I do that?" she says, her voice like gravel.

"It was grief," I says.

"I hardly knew her."

"Grief for a person. Grief for yourself. You don't want to think it, but that could've been you."

I don't want to scare her, that's not the reason I tell her like that. I want to let her know that the woman who rented her flat got killed by mistake. That it wasn't a random-stranger killing, some madman or cokehead out on a spree.

"That was meant to be you," I says.

I tell her because intentional homicide we can do something about, stranger killing is like a bolt out of the blue. How do you catch lightning? How do you know when it's going to strike again?

She stares at me and nods, her mouth getting steady. She's got hold of herself and then some.

"What does it mean?" she says.

"What else can it figure?" I says. "I was warned off the bombing. Twice I was warned off the bombing. Somebody sees me with you. I'm still asking questions. What do they know we got a personal arrangement? Maybe they think I'll get you to remember something you saw but forgot you saw, or heard but forgot you heard. Maybe it's just you saw the guy with the badge."

"I don't know anything I don't know I know," she says, which is a foolish thing to say in a way.

"They see me at the morgue. They see me talking to Pescaro in the delicatessen. They see me trying to identify that Ciccone. They think I won't listen. They think I won't leave it alone, and they think they should stop you before I give you a face to look at."

Pescaro comes in with O'Shea and Rourke. He sees Mary standing next to me and his mouth twitches like he's smiling in relief.

There's uniforms all over the place. The medical examiner himself arrives and stoops by the body.

The neighbors are shooed back to their flats.

"Keep yourselves handy," Pescaro tells them. "An officer or a detective is going to come by sometime tonight and ask a few questions."

"I got to get up in the morning for work," the man with the face like a horse complains. "I got to get my sleep."

"Be grateful," O'Shea says, "that woman ain't going to go to work ever again. She's going to sleep forever."

"Please," Rourke says, "we solicit your cooperation. We'll make it as quick and easy as possible."

Pescaro gives the body another look and comes over to Mary and me. "I thought it was your lady when we got the call," he says.

"It could've been."

"Goddamn you and your Irish curiosity," Pescaro says.

"Goddamn clout and cover-ups," I says.

"You complaining? You're part of it."

He's right. I got nothing to say, but I think it's cruel how things that usually work can go bust, how good things can go bad. I get a funny feeling that, young as I am, the world's changed on me while I wasn't looking.

"I am glad you're all right," Pescaro says to Mary.

"*Now*, will you look into who done this?" I says, a little too sharp.

"Watch yourself, Flannery," he says.

"Because whoever done this, done the bombing," I says.

"We don't know that."

"I think we *would* have known it if we had the chance to match this bullet with the one that killed Helen Caplet, except that bullet is missing."

"Goddammit, Flannery, stay out of this from now on." His eyes flicker to Mary. "It ain't only your ass."

I take Mary's arm at the elbow and steer her through the crowd of cops, who are doing their best to act like they really want to get evidence on whoever did what is laying on the floor, a young woman dead.

Rourke is leaning against the doorjamb, halfway out in the hall.

"Thank you, Rourke," I says.

"Sure, you're welcome," he says, looking vague and surprised.

"I mean really thank you."

"What for?"

"For telling me about the bullet which they found in Helen Caplet."

"You're thanking the wrong person," he says.

"So you don't want my marker?"

"Not for nothing."

My old man looks ten years older sitting at the kitchen table in my flat. Mike's been in plenty of fights in his life, but he ain't never had someone actually commit mayhem on hisself or somebody near and dear. Every now and then, while we talk, he reaches over and squeezes Mary's hand. Tears come up and threaten to spill over, but he fights them back.

He says "sonofabitch," then begs her pardon. He says "Jesus, Mary, and Joseph," then crosses himself.

"Pretty soon, maybe already, whoever done this shooting finds out that Mary Ellen Dunne ain't dead," he says.

"You want I should hang Mary's underwear out on the line along with my shorts so everybody should know we're living together?" I says, snapping at him.

He looks wounded but forgiving, like an old cat what you've kicked off the rug in front of the stove for no reason.

"I mean, if she's living with me and they're worried she's got something to tell, well, then, there's all the more chances for her to remember . . . all the more reason for them to come after her again."

"You do an interview for the paper," Mike says. "You're the party captain in the precinct where these bad things has happened," he says. "We get Delvin to sponsor it. You tell one and all that you're sorry and mad for what some misguided person done at the clinic, which was wrong, though they may have thought it was right, and you'll pray for their soul. You've talked to the people at the clinic, the doctors and nurses, and you've talked to the protesters marching outside. You're convinced that nobody knows nothing."

I stare at my old man, not believing what I'm hearing. He's asking me to beg whoever killed Helen Caplet and Mrs. Klutzman and the nurse who was in Mary's apartment—which might have easily been Mary herself—to leave us alone.

"You go on the television, six-o'clock news, and say the same thing, making sure that everybody understands that nobody knows nothing."

"Like hell," I says. "You want me to roll over for

some people what would kill pregnant girls and old ladies and put a bullet in a nurse?"

"You say that you're a precinct captain worried about his neighborhood and his people, but you ain't a cop, so you'll leave the police work to the cops. You know that, if this somebody is still in the city to be caught, the cops'll catch him."

I lean forward over the oilcloth on the table so far my chin is almost on it, so I'll be sure my old man hears what I got to say since I'm so mad there's a plug in my throat which could choke me. The smell of the oilcloth reminds me of when I was a kid and I'd lean my chin on the table while my mother—God bless her and keep her—trimmed the crust off a pie.

"I was going to let this thing drop. I was going to turn my back on this whore who was going to have a baby scraped out of her belly and an old lady who wanted to hold her hand while they done it, because my Chinaman and another warlord who had an interest asked me to. Before they even see I'm going on about other business, whoever does it goes after a nurse they only think maybe can point the finger. Or, worse, they go after her because they find out she means the world to me and they want to teach me a lesson up front—"

"Hey, Jimmy," my old man says.

"Take a deep breath," Mary says.

"Pescaro called me Delvin's dog. We had some conversation about dogs ourselves, Pop. I said I wasn't a dog. I was wrong. I'm a dog. I'm a junkyard dog. And they're going to find out that I'm as mean as a junkyard dog."

"Shame on you," my old man says. "Shame on me for having a son who'd think Mike Flannery would want a son of his to tuck his tail between his legs and run after somebody's tried to hurt his near and dear."

"You're just after telling me—"

"I tell you to make your public announcements

and maybe keep whoever it is running around like a mad dog cooled out a day or two while we go find out what we can find out."

"Ah, Pop, I'm such a fool, such a fool," I says, and puts my head down on the oilcloth.

Mary puts her hand on my head and it feels like my mother's hand.

16

So I go on television and say my piece. And I talk to the reporters in Delvin's office, while he stands in the corner and grins, and say it again. I hope that it does the job. I hope whoever it is thought they was killing Mary thinks I'm scared blue.

After the interview with the ladies and gentlemen of the press, I invite Jackie Boyle for coffee when nobody's looking or on the eary. He's a columnist for the *Sun-Times*, not as hot as Kupcinet or Royko, so he's more amenable to doing favor for favor.

I take a handful of change from my pocket and run them from hand to hand. There is mostly nickels.

"Hinting for a handout?" Boyle says.

I take a nickel and put it on the table between us. "I'm a poor man, but I'm a man who pays in advance."

"If that ain't a nickel, what is it?" he says.

"My marker."

He puts his finger on the nickel and pulls it toward him maybe six inches, which means he ain't making no commitment.

"I want you should check the sheriff's list of who-ever holds a part-time deputy's gun and a badge."

"So you was blowing smoke," he says.

I put another nickel on the table. His finger hovers over it but don't touch it.

"Keep it to yourself. I don't want anybody to know. That's why I don't check the list myself."

His finger don't move. We're staring into each other's eyes.

"Somebody thought they was killing a woman who's everything to me," I says.

His finger falls down on the nickel and he pulls it in like before.

"You know how many goddamned names is probably on such a list?"

"I think I'm only looking for a badge-holder from Velletri's Twenty-fifth and the number on the badge is three, maybe four, digits with a two in the middle."

"Jesus Christ," he says, and flicks the two nickels back at me. "You're talking about the mob, the members of which could be carrying more tin than all the detectives on the force put together."

"Don't kid me. They don't even bother. Why should they? They don't need no tin. But there are those who are mob-connected or politically connected who like to belly up to the bar in the policemen's saloons. Who like to chase the calls just like the fire buffs who answer every alarm."

I put a quarter on the table in the middle of the two nickels. I'm giving him plenty of credit with me. He knows what a precinct captain connected like I'm connected can do for a man who writes a column. Still he hesitates.

"You got any idea who you're looking for?" he says.

"Not a clue. I'm just collecting pieces. I'm just looking for one and one and one and one, I should maybe make at least two."

I put another quarter down.

He scoops the change up.

"I'll pay for the coffees," he says.

"Ain't it lucky this place only charges thirty cents a cup?" I says.

"So, I'll leave the tip," he says, and drops another fifteen cents on the table.

*   *   *

My old man comes back to my flat from doing some errands for me and throws down a list on which I've written the names of everybody I can think of who might have had knowledge of the bullet in Helen Caplet, and who might have thought to do me the favor by calling me and giving me the information.

"I done like you told me," he says. "I sound out Benedetto and Jackson and all these others. Nobody cops even when I say that you're ready to owe the one who done you the favor. Who doesn't want a free marker? I even do the number on Pescaro. At first he looks at me like I'm getting senile, then he tries to make something of it, but I double-talk him and slip out of it."

The phone rings. I wonder does a phone ring a certain way when it's got important things to deliver.

"Helen Caplet is not Helen Caplet," the same whispery voice says. "Her prints made her, but the cops won't tell you that. She's Helen Brickhouse and she used to live over to Cicero. Three-five-nine Mercer Street, top floor."

I write it down on the oilcloth.

"What do you want?" I says. "Nobody does nothing for nothing."

"Figure it out," he says, and hangs up.

"Who's doing us these favors?" my old man asks.

"Maybe they ain't doing us any favors. Maybe they're doing themselves a favor," I says.

17

There are parts of Chicago that are very tough, going all the way back to the days when Capone and his mob ruled until Dever pushed him out of the city into Cicero, where, even today, anything goes. My own Twenty-seventh, with Skid Row in the middle, is no convent, but Cicero makes it look like a girl's school at least. It's Mafia, and no bones about it. Nobody can fart—you should excuse my French—in Cicero, the family don't hear it and smell it. This family is not the same thing as you mean when you talk about your family or even what I mean when I talk about my family.

I find the three-story frame house on Mercer Street with no trouble. It's a neighborhood which is respectable, but poor, filled with Polish and Irish who made the move out of Chicago to what looked like greener pastures two generations ago, then ran out of steam.

The lock on the two doors downstairs don't work, so I don't have to use the buzzer. I'm able to walk up the stairs and knock on the door.

A man in his underwear shirt and suspenders, with a beer belly hanging out, comes to the door with a newspaper in one hand. He looks at me and says, "Yeah?"

"Mr. Brickhouse?"

"Yeah?" he says.

"My name's Jimmy Flannery," I says, "and I come to talk to you about your daughter, Helen."

"I ain't got no daughter," he says.

Down at the end of the dark hall behind him a worn-out woman stands in the light from the kitchen. She's wearing a wraparound house dress and wiping her hands on a dish towel.

"Please, Marty," she says, like a prayer.

He leans back like he wants to get a better look at me, then unfolds the paper and takes a look.

"You're this guy?" he says.

"That's me."

"A celebrity's come to call, Flo," he says. "Well, come on in. You're letting in a draft."

I follow him down the hall, and I step back twenty-five years in time. It's just like the flat I grew up in when I was little until we moved into a house. The bathroom's the first on the left. There's a closed door to the second bedroom on the right. Then, one side of the hall, there's a dining room and a parlor through a doorway on the right. The sliding doors to the parlor is closed so there won't be so much house to heat. I guess the dining-room door to the second bedroom will be closed, too, unless they got other kids besides Helen. On the left is the doorway into the kitchen with old scrub tubs and a kitchen table and chairs in the middle. There's oilcloth on the table. Next to the refrigerator is the door to the main bedroom, which is also closed.

"Sit down," Flo says to me, blushing, as shy as a bride. As tired out and faded as she is, I can still see why Helen was so pretty under the hardness and paint. These flats is filled with women you could match with any woman on the television shows except for the way the cards fell. "You want coffee . . ." she says.

"My pleasure," I says.

". . . and a piece of coffee cake? It ain't home-made but it was fresh from the bakery this morning."

I take a bite of the cake and a swallow of the

coffee. It's the hospitality of the house and it ain't
right to start talking about what I come to talk about
until it's out of the way. It's hard for Brickhouse to sit
there letting me have the coffee and cake because
he's afraid I come with bad news. He don't know
how bad.

"So, all right," he says.

"A girl named Helen Caplet was . . ."

"Oh, no!" Flo says, and gasps like she's drowning.

". . . killed in an explosion in a clinic over to Sperry
Avenue in my precinct, which is in the Twenty-
seventh ward."

After the word "killed," Flo sits there staring at me
as though I'm a man who just put an ice pick through
her heart and she can't understand why I would do
such a thing.

"So what is this Helen Caplet to do with us?"
Brickhouse says.

"They match her prints. She's your daughter, Helen
Brickhouse."

Brickhouse stares at me, too, but he don't blink.
The rims of his eyes are turning red, and mottled
color is spreading over his heavy neck and chin. He's
about fifty-five and I'm afraid he might be going to
have a heart attack.

"What kind of a clinic?" he says in a voice which is
tied with a cord.

"A clinic where girls which has got themselves in
trouble can get help."

"I told you what she was, Flo. I told you," he says,
but he don't look at his wife. "You wouldn't believe
me when I told you what she was and why I didn't
want her back in this house."

"My God, Marty, not what she *was*, what she might
of become."

Women see the difference that men often don't.
Helen was her little girl, with shiny hair and rosy
cheeks and a baby's innocence, and always would be,

no matter what else the grown-up Helen ever might have become. For Brickhouse, all Helen gave him for his hopes was a paper bag full of busted dreams and shame.

"She was a whore, Flo," Brickhouse says. Then the tears start pouring out of his eyes. I never see such a thing. His face don't move, he still don't blink, and the water just rolls down his red cheeks like a flood, catching and sparkling in the stubble on his chin. He don't make a sound. It's one of the most terrible things I ever see.

"My God, my little baby, Helen. My little Pudding," he says. He gets up. "I want to thank you for coming and telling us," he says like he's minding his manners. "Where is she?"

"Over to county morgue."

"Can I get her?"

"Anytime you want."

He leaves the kitchen and goes down the hall. I hear a door open and close.

"He'll lay on her bed and hug her rag doll," Flo says. "He don't think I know what he does. Is your coffee hot?"

"It's hot."

"Sure it is. Why wouldn't it be? I just now poured it, didn't I? I feel awful. There's something in my chest that feels like it's going to choke me."

"You want I should call a doctor?"

"Oh, no, people like us don't call a doctor for things like this. It's easier to die, anyway, ain't it?"

"Mrs. Brickhouse," I says, "I want you should help me if you can."

"How?"

"I wonder if Helen ever told you she met a man . . ."

"How could she tell me anything? Her father forbid her ever to step foot in this house . . ."

". . . and made a special friend?"

". . . or even meet me on the street or in a coffee shop."

"Did she tell you she met a man who she fell in love with?"

"Can't you hear me what I'm telling you?"

"Mrs. Brickhouse, mothers and daughters has been talking to each other, no matter what the old man says, for a thousand years."

"All right. What could it matter now, anyway? Helen called me on the phone sometimes when she knew her father wouldn't be home. We'd meet and have a piece of a pie and a coffee somewheres."

"Was there a man?"

"Yes, she said there was. This man wanted Helen to stop doing what she was doing."

"That's how he met her?"

"I don't know. He was married, she said, but he wanted to set her up. He couldn't do it right away, but he was ready to leave his wife. That would've made her father hit the roof, too. He don't go to church, but he believes in the faith. He don't believe in a daughter running around with a married man."

"Was this married man making promises?"

"I told Helen not to believe him. I told her men always make promises they don't mean to keep."

"But she kept seeing him?"

"What was wrong with that? She was seeing different men all the time anyway, wasn't she?"

"He sets her up in a flat? He pays the bills?"

"Oh, no. But, with this one, she says they go out to the lakefront and go sailing and take bicycle rides in Grant Park. At least with him it ain't like she's doing it just for the money."

She looks at me as if to say what damned difference did it make what you did it for? It's all buying and selling, one way or another.

Then her expression gets soft and she says, "Once last summer he took her on a long weekend to Atlantic City. He bought her a long summer dress and a hat. They had cold drinks with gin and pineapple juice. She didn't like the taste much. But it must have been grand."

"What month did they go?"

"June."

"You know the week?"

"The first one."

"You're sure."

"Pretty nearly sure. Helen's birthday was on the third and she said he took her to Atlantic City like it was a present."

"She bring back any pictures?"

At first I don't think she's going to admit it. She's already telling me more than she wants to tell a stranger. But who else has she got to show the pictures of her baby in her summer dress? She gets up and goes into her bedroom and comes back with three snapshots wrapped in a napkin.

It's a souvenir napkin from the Hotel Beau Rivage in Atlantic City, New Jersey, a daughter's gift to a mother who'd never have a chance to wear a summer dress and stroll along the boardwalk in a resort city on the sea.

She tosses a glance at the hallway, afraid that maybe her husband will come creeping up on us while she's showing me pictures she ain't supposed to have. She lays them out one by one.

They're pictures taken from far back so all the dress will show, but I can see the girl in the picture is the girl who was Helen Caplet. The man with her is smiling with a lot of very white teeth. He's got an Italian face which is very dark or he's got a tan and he's got slicked-back black hair. I think I know him from somewhere, but I can't put my finger on it. Then I remember what Mary said about the guy in the corridor. He *does* look like Valentino.

They look happy. I can see the front of the hotel

in the background with its name above the entrance in pink letters.

"Can I have one of these?" I asks.

Flo hesitates for a second, then she says, "Does it matter which?"

I says, "No."

She sorts the three pictures out on the table, shoving them around like she's working the shell game. Then she pushes one toward me. I put it in my pocket.

"Thanks for this, and the coffee and cake."

"Why do you want the picture?" Flo says.

"I think this man could have been responsible for the explosion which hurt your Helen," I says.

"I hope you do it to him," Flo says. She sees me to the door. "Mr. Flannery?" Flo says. "You got kids?"

"No. I ain't even married yet."

"Don't have kids. They'll break your heart."

18

I have the half of the picture with Helen's boyfriend blown up to a three-by-four. It's grainy, but at least you can see the shape of the eyes and mouth a little better.

The first ones I show it to is my father and Mary.

"That's the man who showed me the badge in the corridor of the clinic."

"Would you say that was him if you was under oath?" I says.

She hesitates a tick. "Maybe not," she says. "A person's raised not wanting to accuse anyone, not get into trouble, so that's a very difficult question to answer."

"Think about it."

"So, if it was a lineup, I'd probably say yes. If it was a trial, and life and death, I'm not so sure."

"It doesn't matter right this minute. Whatever you have to say wouldn't be enough anyway. Not even for an arrest. But I think I got my fingers on the end of the string which is going to unravel the whole ball."

Delvin holds the blowup between his thumb and finger.

"I ask you to mind your business. You don't mind your business," he says. "Why is that? Don't you like your job?"

"With all respect, this is the guy who killed a young

pregnant whore, an old lady, and an innocent party who was a nurse."

"You got eyewitnesses to these allegations?"

"I got reasonable suspicions."

"The cops share these reasonable suspicions of . yours?"

"The cops have a desire to do what they're told to do. This is a desire they share with a lot of other people," I says, which ain't very smart, since Delvin don't have to be smart hisself to know exactly what I'm getting at.

"If you was a cop, I'd tell you where you could stick your reasonable suspicions, but you ain't a cop," he says. "You're a buttinsky, a guy who sticks his nose in places he shouldn't stick his nose. A guy who doesn't listen to them who has his best interests at heart. To them who's done him favors and who's asking a little favor in return."

"I'm asking you, Mr. Delvin, who asked you to tell me to stop poking around?"

"Which you don't do," he shouts, getting red in the face.

"Which I was *going* to do, but which I'm not going to do now because the nurse who this somebody murdered could've been my lady."

"Oh," he says like I stepped on his toe and he was saying ouch. He's got nothing to say to a man who's telling him this is something so personal political loyalty don't even figure into it anymore.

"So?" I says.

He hands the picture back to me. "I don't know this guy. When I'm asked to tell you—ask you—to forget about the bombing over to the abortion clinic on Sperry, I figure it's because there are people who might not agree with such a violent way of making a protest, but who do not want the perpetrator—who did not mean to hurt anyone, just a building—to go to jail for having fumble fingers."

"You don't ask anything else?"

"If that's a sneaky way of passing judgment on the favor I done, you better say it straight out."

"No," I says, shaking my head. "I'm just feeling mean."

"I give you that. I'll also give you . . ."

"Give me the name of the man who asked the favor."

". . . a piece of advice. Before, I asked you forget about this thing. Now I got to beg you to walk away. It's going to get . . ."

"I don't need the name. I know it's Vito Velletri."

". . . very bloody for you, I think, if you don't. I'm giving you this advice because I love you like my own son."

The biggest con is the one that goes, "I'm telling you this because I love you." It's just the same as the one that goes, "This is going to hurt me more than it will you."

Another thing you learn, if you learn anything, is that very few people know about how hard you're trying to be yourself—and they don't want to know about it if being yourself interferes with them being theirselves.

I didn't have to ask Delvin who asked him to do the cover-up, to give the word to Pescaro to ease off the clinic bombing, to tell me I should mind my business. I already know it's Delvin's fellow warlord Velletri. I asked him so he could get hisself untangled from the mess his favor helped to cause. To clean his shoes. To let him know I'm getting to the bottom of this particular cesspool any way I can, no matter how long it takes, no matter who tries to stop me.

I give him a chance to be a *mensch*—a Yiddish word which means a stand-up guy—but he don't take it. Delvin is getting old and soft.

I'm not going to give Velletri the same chance, because he's not my Chinaman, and all I'll get from him is orders to back off otherwise he will break my arms and legs.

19

The laying out of Helen Bernadette Catherine Brickhouse in McCardle's Funeral Home is nothing like the laying out of Mrs. Rose Sonia Klutzman in her living room.

Helen has got on a dress that would suit a child getting graduated from high school, a pink thing of layered chiffon that makes me sad for her. Here she grew up with all them lies about how to cop a happy future, a husband, kids, and a split-level over to Park Ridge—even if it is a Republican suburb. But all the kid's got to do is look at where she is, what she come from, and what are the odds of getting somewhere else, to know she's got to do more than pass her civics class and take a bath once a day if she hopes to get out of a life like her mother's life. Which to her is as dingy as dishwater. Which to her is no better than being dead.

Maybe she traded lies for wrong ideas. But, for a while there, when some customer convinced her she was more than just a whore to him, when she let herself get pregnant, before she was told to get rid of the baby or else—maybe it wasn't even a threat, maybe it was just a payoff, some cash, and a promise of later—she must have figured her game plan was working.

Now they had her back in school, looking like their idea of a virgin, and it was like she'd never hoped, never tried, never even lived a woman's life.

Flo Brickhouse is sitting in the first row, dressed in

her best and wearing her hat. Some old female relatives and neighbors, wearing black as though the century had never bothered turning, is clustered around her. Some of these old crows was probably the same ones what pecked out Helen's eyes with their sharp tongues. That made Flo's life a misery with their whispers.

I go over to Flo Brickhouse and make my condolences.

"I'm very sorry for your loss, Mrs. Brickhouse," I says. "I never knew your Helen, but I see what a pretty girl she was and I know she had a sweet soul."

The old ladies in black is eyeing me like they will bust if Flo don't tell them who this stranger is coming in to a family wake like this. They're wondering am I somebody from Helen's other, terrible, sinful life.

"Thank you, Mr. Flannery. It's good of you to come to pay your respects when you're under no obligation."

"The misfortune which befell her," I says, "happened in my precinct, and that's enough. Mary Ellen Dunne, the nurse who was in the building when it happened, wanted to come, but she's on shift at Passavant."

"Thank her for the intention."

"She'll make a point to come to the service if it's anywhere near possible."

"Saint Jude's, the little church on—"

"I know where it is."

"Two o'clock day after tomorrow."

"We'll be there. I'll just go say a prayer now, will I? There's people waiting to give you their strength."

I go up to the coffin and kneel down on the little stool. I look into Helen's face. The mortician's paint and powder makes her look even harder than when she was laying in the morgue like a busted doll.

"You take care," I says, because I'm not very good at praying.

I see Marty Brickhouse come from the hall and stand in the doorway with his hands folded in front of his belly. He's wearing his good suit and it makes him look out of place. I know he's just come upstairs from the basement where there's a room where the men hang out to smoke and pass a bottle.

I cross myself and go over to give him my sympathy. He stares at me like he's going to fight with me. I don't know why. Whatever, whoever, reminds him of what his Pudding was before she died is somebody to punish, I suppose. Then he relaxes and it looks for a minute like he's going to cry again. I don't think I can stand that so I says, "Is there a drink on the premises?"

"Oh, sure," he says, like I've reminded him about his manners. There's ancient custom about things like this. The way it goes, he'd have to offer hospitality to the devil. "Come downstairs with me."

In the room there's half a dozen guys look just like Brickhouse sitting and standing around smoking. They got hands like my father, heavy and scarred, yellow with nicotine, and very unhappy when they got nothing to do. Brickhouse gets a bottle from the potted palm. I only wet my lips because I hate the stuff. I think maybe we'll talk, though about what and why I don't know, but instead we just sit there staring at the potted palm.

In a little while I go upstairs and stand in the doorway looking at everybody who comes in. I hang around until they close the place up, waiting for a certain somebody to show.

Delvin comes to pay his respects and so does Vito Velletri, but I don't see nobody who looks like Valentino.

20

I left the car at home in case Mary needs it, so I take the el back to my precinct. I got six blocks to walk through the empty streets. I tuck my house keys between my fingers in case some mugger should come at me I can cut his cheek. I step along calm and easy watching my shadow in front of me every time I put another streetlamp behind me. I watch the alleys and look for motion behind the windows of parked cars. Even so I don't see where they come from.

I'm on the floor in the back of a car with somebody's shoe on my neck before I know what hits me. It's a black shoe, well-polished and with a pointy toe. A dancer's shoe. A gonif's shoe. A shoe which belongs to a man who knows how to damage a man's ribs with a kick.

There's two other guys in front, the driver and another guy who's annoyed that they was called away out of some warm nightclub to do somebody a service at this time of night.

"I don't like this, Connie," this one says. "I was doing great with Hester. I never see such tits—"

"Shut up," Connie says.

"We was going back to her place when the call come."

"I don't tell you again."

We drive for a while. I try to count one hundred and one, one hundred and two. If I can count the seconds and if I can estimate how fast we're going,

then I can figure how many miles we've traveled.
Then, when I get loose, I'll draw a circle of that
diameter around the spot where they picked me up.
Someplace inside that circle will be the place where
they're taking me. I will find it later on and track
these bastards down and see that what they do to me
is done to them.

Except they got to travel in a straight line, and
except I find it very hard to keep on counting with
somebody's foot grating on my cheek, and except
I'm afraid that maybe I'll be in no condition to do
nothing to nobody because I'll be dead.

Every once in a while I hear ice cubes rattle in a
glass when Connie takes a swallow of the drink which
he was probably drinking when they was called away
to do this job on me. I'm so thirsty I could lick a wet
stone.

The tires rattle over old cobbles and railroad tracks,
so I know we're in a section of the city which is
empty after dark.

The car stops somewhere not too far from the
main railroad yard. I can hear them making up the
freight trains, which sometimes is three hundred
cars long, the couplings smashing iron to iron like I
remember when I was a kid.

The guy in front gets out and leaves the door
open. I hear the rattle of a chain and the creak of a
gate. The car pulls ahead and he jumps back in. The
sound of the engine changes like we're driving
through a long tunnel. The car stops again.

"Let me get out first," the guy with his foot in my
face says. "Then you come out of the car, Flannery.
Keep your hands at your sides. Keep your eyes in
front of you. I don't want you should try to look at
our faces. You understand that?"

He takes his foot off my neck and steps out of the
car. For a wild minute I think I can maybe rise up,
give the driver a clout alongside the ear, jump over

into the front seat, shove him out the door, and take the hell off. It gives me a minute of joy, then I manage to uncramp myself and crawl out of the car, practically falling on my head.

We're in the middle of a junkyard. It's like the way the world will look when tomorrow catches up with us and we drown in garbage. It's mostly the smashed bodies of cars, some wrecks of the road, some old bones tossed away. They're piled up like monuments. I take a step and turn my head a little because I don't know what else to do and I'm very frightened. I get a look at Connie in the light of the moon.

Whatever's left in his glass hits me in the face. He smashes the glass on the bricks. One of them comes around from my blind side and slams a punch into my gut, which makes me get sick on the ground. Some of it splashes on Connie's shoe.

"Oh, for Christ's sake," he says, and he stoops down and wipes the toe of his shoe with the bar napkin with which he was holding the glass.

I'm on my knees watching him do it like it's the most interesting thing I seen all week.

Something slams into the back of my neck, under the ear. I don't remember going down.

When I come to, the car is gone and I'm cramped up on the filthy ground, hunched over my knees, my legs pushed out like a frog, keeping me from falling over even though I was knocked out. I stick a hand under my coat and feel my ribs. They ain't busted. I run a hand over my face. My nose and teeth ain't broken. I'm just stiff from kneeling there. I reach out for the dirty napkin which Connie has thrown away after wiping his shoe.

All they wanted to do was give me a scare. All they wanted to do was tell me that enough was enough and if I . . .

A Doberman as big as a pony comes charging down one of the alleys between the walls of rusting steel and iron. There's enough light from the moon that I can see his red eyes and the way his fangs shine.

I stagger up to my feet. It hurts like hell to move so quick, but I know it's going to hurt a hell of a lot more if I don't find some high ground and that animal gets his teeth into me. I scramble and scrap my way up a pile of rusted cars. Glass from their busted windows tears my clothes and cuts my hands and knees. It feels like every time I climb two feet, something gives way and I slip back one. The dog is leaping at me, not like a dumb animal bouncing up and down without gathering itself, but like some-body with a plan. The jumps is timed to give him the best shot at my foot or leg every time one comes close enough for him to maybe catch hold.

Once he gets my pants cuff, and when I drag my leg up, I drag him along with me. He lets go and plants his four paws on a flat place. He can make my throat with one try if he wants. I'm laying bellydown against the scrap metal, afraid to move in case I slide right down to the ground again, afraid not to be-cause if I don't the dog will have me for supper.

I kick out just as he leaps and catch him in the chest. He bounces off and goes falling to the ground all in a scramble, tangled up in some upholstery and headliner webbing. But the contact is enough to send me sliding off the hill, too. I get my feet under me and hit the ground running. I head toward the gate.

When I look back over my shoulder, the Doberman's got hisself together again and is coming after me. The thing that scares me most is that he don't make a sound. He's a fighter who don't waste his breath on threats.

There's a donkey engine that runs a crane stand-ing in the aisle between mountains of cars, close to the chain-link fence which has got razor wire coiled along the top. I jump into the cab and kick the engine over. It catches and roars. The dog leaps at me in the cab and I kick him again under the jaw so he goes tumbling back, hitting the ground rolling like a wrestler and coming back at me right away. But at least I got time to throw the lever to swing the crane and get out of the cab and up the boom. Spotlights start popping on all over the yard. I make like a monkey and I'm at the top of the boom when the crane slams into the fence.

I go over and run down the dark, wet street toward the black shapes of big warehouses while the dog bites the steel mesh and yells at me, begging me to come back and fight like a man.

21

When I stop running, I start to shake. When I stop shaking, I look for a handkerchief to wipe the sweat off my face. I find the dirty napkin in my pocket. I must have shoved it in there without knowing I was doing it when the Doberman came at me. I open it up and see that it's from a club which I know over to the Loop. I remember that there's a dancer who works there who's got size forties up front. I don't know that her name is Hester, but I'm willing to bet on it.

I'm presentable if not clean by the time I get to the Jambo Club. There's pictures of several of the attractions outside. One of them is Hester Prime. I don't know if that's supposed to be a takeoff on the name of the woman who wore the scarlet letter in the book of the same name, which is written by Nathaniel Hawthorne, or if it has to do with meat packing and grading. In Chicago it means probably the second.

The bouncer at the door gives me the eye and says, "Are you drunk and have you made a mess of yourself?"

"I'm not drunk. Smell my breath," I says. "I was mugged. I'm so upset I would maybe like a drink at your bar before I go home."

All the time I'm looking over his shoulder so I shouldn't come face to face with Connie. I'm worried that I won't even know it if I come face to face with the other two.

The bouncer steps aside and I'm able to get to the bar, which is off to one side at the back of the club, without showing myself. The floor show is going on, and a line of girls is high-kicking and singing in shrill voices like peahens about "happy days are here again." Chicago can't get over Prohibition. When the citizens of Chicago go out to have fun, all the women want to be flappers and all the men want to be gangsters. It's like after Capone everything is downhill.

The club ain't all that crowded, but it's crowded enough. I order a rye and ginger ale, which I'm not going to drink, and start searching the crowd table by table, looking for two guys what look dandy. I figure the driver is just a driver and not one of the boys when it comes to fun and frolic.

There is plenty of types, but I don't see Connie. Maybe they decide to go home and call it a night after feeding the dog.

Then I see this blonde in a dressing gown, which tells me she's a performer sitting with a customer before she goes on. There's only the two of them at the table. The man she's sitting with looks like one of them water rats which comes up from the lake, slick and sure of hisself, his little mustache twitching every time he thinks of what he'd like to do with them things the woman is practically resting on the table.

The dancers high-kick one last time and go shuffling off to Buffalo off the floor. The barker comes out and says that Hester Prime will now take off her clothes, which is what she does best. The blonde bounces up off the chair and makes for the door, which gives her the chance to take off the dressing gown and come out ready to strip. It's very old-fashioned.

I lean over sideways and says to the bartender, "Is that Hester's brother from Philadelphia she's sitting with?"

"That's Choo-Choo Torello."

"What's a Choo-Choo Torello?"

"He throws people under trains," the bartender says.

"Who does he do this service for?" I says.

The bartender walks away in case I want to know more about Choo-Choo Torello.

Choo-Choo is watching Hester and I think maybe she'll drown him in all that white body or choke him to death with the powder she fans herself with before the night is over. I also think he won't mind a bit.

When Hester shows every inch she can show and struts off the floor in a blue spot, Choo-Choo gets up and hurries over toward the men's room, stopping along the way to pay the waiter so he shouldn't waste a minute getting out of there with Hester.

When he comes through the door and steps into the first stall, I'm in the second one. I peek through the spyhole which somebody had drilled in the partition, and see him take off his suit jacket and hang it on the hook. Then he drops his trousers.

"Hey, Choo-Choo," I whisper.

He don't turn a hair.

"Listen, faggot," he says, "you get your eye away from that hole or I'm going to poke it out with a knife."

"Hey, Choo-Choo," I says, "you only think you're tough. I'm going to tell . . ."

He starts to reach for the gun which he's got tucked in a holster under his arm pit.

". . . your boss you like boys."

"You asshole," he says, "DiBella knows better than that."

I step out of my stall just as he's pulling out the gun and getting up from the stool. I slam the door to his stall back as hard as I can while he's in a bare-assed crouch, one hand with a gun and the other pulling up his shorts. He falls down between the toilet and the wall. He don't even get to see me before I walk out the door.

22

I told you something about politics in Chicago, now I'll tell you a little about what is called high society. There's not a hell of a lot of "old money" around here; it's all been made two, at most three, generations ago by people like Cornelius Vanderbilt, who ran a garbage scow; Swift, who got his start peddling raw meat from a pushcart; and Marshall Field, who owned a dry-goods store.

Chicago's got a social register. I'm told that actors and actresses are welcome, but people of the Jewish faith are not unless they marry somebody already in the register.

There are exclusive clubs like the Chicago Club and the Casino Club, and a lot of charity doings for things like the Lyric Opera, the University of Chicago, the Junior League, St. Luke's Medical Center, and the Brookfield Zoo. Everybody appreciates these good works.

High society would like to claim some political power in the city, but the truth is that the people down to City Hall don't really give a rat's ass about what these rich people have to say or what they would like to see knocked down or built up. They like their campaign contributions, but there's even something all cockeyed about that, since these rich businessmen register Republican but contribute to the Democratic machine to buy what favors they hope to buy.

Society women give a lot of parties and are probably useful in that way, bringing Democrats together with Republicans and Liberals, the corporation heads with the union bosses, the real-estate tycoons with the clergy, the art patrons with the sports buffs, and the mob leaders with the bankers.

Jennifer "Poppsie" Hanneman was born into a family what ran a hot-dog stand in the Tenth ward which was frequented by a lot of the steel workers. She performed in some chorus lines on the Loop and performed on her back in a nice little flat she bought herself on the lakefront. She married into the big Hanneman cold-cut fortune in the person of Barney "Knockwurst"—which nobody called him to his face—Hanneman, who was twice her age. So she was a widow not long after the wedding. She's very good at giving parties.

Poppsie lives in a Lakeview Avenue duplex overlooking the park. I'm lucky in the lobby because the old guard on duty is Danny Maroon, who's been on nights at the building for twenty years and has a memory for names and faces I should be so lucky to possess.

He remembers me right away, even though it's been five years since I used to come visiting and stay the night . . . but that's another story.

"It's you, is it, Mr. Flannery?"

"It's me."

"Are you back?"

"Just to have a drink," I says. "Dinner should be over by now, don't you think?"

"You wasn't invited?"

"Just for something after," I says, lying with a look which my mother—God rest her soul—used to say would fool the devil.

"Enjoy yourself, Mr. Flannery," he says.

"You, too, Mr. Maroon," I says.

I take the elevator up to the top floor. It opens up into a hall bigger than my flat with nothing in it but a painting at one end, a mirror at the other, and a little table, which has got a silver tray on it, next to the door facing the elevator.

Poppsie's butler opens up. He's not the butler I once knew. He gives me a quick once-over. His eyes is like mice peeking into my pockets. I don't pass the test. He does the eyebrow thing. I think maybe everybody in the world learns to look down their noses except me.

"I've come to call on Mrs. Hanneman," I says.

"Madam is giving a dinner party," he says.

"I ain't hungry," I says, "and won't stay. But I want a word with Jennifer—"

"I'm afraid—"

"Jenny will want to know I'm here. Go whisper in Poppsie's ear that James Flannery is here or I'll make a mess on the rug."

He turns his back on me and stalks down the corridor toward the room from which there is coming a lot of conversation and a lot of light. I'm right behind him. The rugs is so thick he can't hear me and he ain't street-smart enough to feel me at his back.

When he stops in the doorway of the dining room, which looks like the Hall of Mirrors in the Palace of Versailles like I seen in that picture about Wilson on the late-late show, I go right on past him.

Poppsie looks at me. One second I think she's going to laugh and the next she's going to cry and the next she's going to get mad and tell every man in the room to get up from their dinner and break my teeth.

She's got about thirty people sitting around the long table which is covered with enough china and silver to set me and Mary up in a house in the suburbs with two cars in the garage. The women are in long dresses and most of the men are wearing dinner jackets. They're going to some opening at the

Art Institute after this little supper. I found that out when I chased down the man I want to see with a few phone calls.

A few of the people I know, like Wilson Frost, the black ward leader of the Thirty-fourth over to the South Side; my old friend George Lurgan from the Fourteenth; and Jerry Kilian from the First, which has the Loop for a heart. I also know Joe Medill, the columnist from the *Trib* and Barry Locker from Channel Two.

Most of the people are looking at me, with my bloody hands and my dirty suit, like I'm some kind of freak or some kook entertainer like them birthday greeters who come around and dance or sing you a song. The women got these nice little smiles pasted on their faces like they're hoping Poppsie ain't gone too far this time and rung in a male stripper or something. A couple of the men are sliding back their chairs because they see the butler is in some distress that I got by him and are about to throw me out even if it means getting their cuffs dirty.

Only two is really hard-eyeing me. One is Smith Jarwolski, the police superintendent who's wearing his dress uniform, and the other is Carmine DiBella, who's rumored to be the top man in the syndicate. Nobody knows for sure because the new-style mobsters keep a very low profile and can be mistaken for a banker or broker very easy.

For some reason, as nervous as I am, it's interesting to me to see the difference in the way these two men make threatening faces at me. Jarwolski has thrown out his chest and pushed his head forward, with his hands clenched on the table like he's ready to punch. He makes a face like a baboon, showing me some teeth and a corrugated forehead. DiBella's hands are still on the tablecloth, almost as fine and white as the Irish linen, and it's only his eyes that tell me I should leave before I'm dead.

Before anybody can do anything, Poppsie stands up and flutters her hands like she's very upset to see a friend in such a state. Like I'm a crazy patient and she's a visiting nurse.

"Bring Mr. Flannery a chair, Carpenter," she says to the butler, who does a quick change with his face. One minute he's outraged with me, the next he's very concerned about my well-being.

"Whatever has happened to you, James?" Poppsie says in that voice she puts on which sounds like a flute, not the least bit anxious that maybe I'm there about to do something which will give the secret away that I've been in this penthouse and in her bed on more than one occasion. She looks like a flower, but she's as tough as a weed.

"No, thanks, Mrs. Hanneman," I says. "I'm not staying long."

"You must have a drink," she says. "Will a whiskey do?"

She throws a glance at Carpenter, who takes a step toward the cut-glass decanters on the sideboard.

"No, thanks, I don't drink spirits," I says, which I don't, except maybe a beer on a hot day at a picnic. I admire how she done that. With one little remark she establishes the fact—for anyone who cares to look the scene over later on—that she knows the ruffian who crashes into her party, but knows him only in the most casual way. Like she met me at a Democratic fund-raiser where she sat with the precinct workers and shared corned beef and cabbage or a rubber chicken.

"I'm sorry I come busting into your party this way, Mrs. Hanneman, but I can't think of no other way to keep myself from getting very badly hurt, maybe killed," I says.

She gives a little gasp, which is also an act because Poppsie wouldn't let out a yell if she saw somebody cut up with a chainsaw. Then I see that maybe I'm all wrong about that. There's a mist in her eyes and I realize that she wasn't lying when she told me that there was no future together for two people, one who'd climbed out of the mud puddle and the other who was still in it making pies, but that she cared for me too much to have me for a toy.

"If your life's being threatened, Mr. Flannery, bring it to the attention of the police in the right way," Jarwolski says.

"Well, Superintendent Jarwolski," I says, "I think it's best that I bring it to the attention of the man who ordered me thrown to the dogs."

I look at DiBella, and his mouth twitches a little like he's amused, but I think it's because he's in a rage with me.

"Is that an accurate statement of fact, or is it just a colorful means of expression?" he says.

"It's what happened to me an hour ago. Three men, two of which I got the names of, Angie and Connie . . ."

"Those are the names of women," he says.

". . . which are Italian, and which work for you, Mr. DiBella, throw me into the back of a car, drive me to a junkyard, punch me in the stomach, and leave me to make the acquaintance of a dog which is as mean as any dog I've ever seen."

"But you were meaner?" DiBella says.

"Just faster. And I hope I'm also smarter, Mr. DiBella. Which is why I don't go to the police, but come here to tell you in public that I don't appreciate you siccing your dogs—them with two legs or four—onto me, and I want you should stop."

"Shall we all stop, Mr. Flannery?" he says as cool as ice, which don't mean he admits having had done what was done, but sounds like he means he's trying to calm down a crazy man and get him the hell out of Poppsie's so they can have their dessert.

"No, Mr. DiBella, I won't stop. How big can this favor be that you're doing for somebody? Can something which isn't a profit to you be so important that three people should die? It's easy to think you can do anything you want with a snap of the fingers like you was the godfather. I get to thinking like that when somebody wants I should have a shade tree cut down because it's spoiling the view or get the water turned on because the toilet won't flush. I'm not coming at you, Mr. DiBella. I'm coming at the man who did the killing."

The flesh around the corners of his mouth and the sides of his nose is so white it's like it's dead of the frost.

"It sounds like you're threatening me, Flannery," he says in a soft voice. "It sounds like you're threatening me in front of my friends. Are you insulting my honor? Should I stand for your insults?"

"I'm just taking out an insurance policy, is all," I says. "If I'm right about what I say, these people are witnesses and maybe you won't do anything to hurt me because they'll know you done it. If I'm wrong about what I say, so you shrug it off because you're a very powerful man and . . ."

When I hesitate he bites it off. "And what are you, Mr. Flannery?"

"A junkyard dog," I says.

"I'll see you to the door," Poppsie says, letting everyone know that she's a mountain of good manners even in the face of such a lout as me. Also she wants to make sure I go out the door.

I let her turn me with just a wave of her hand like the junkyard dog what just growled and showed his teeth is nothing but a puppy in her hands. She waves Carpenter off and he stays put, so we're at the front door alone for a minute.

"My god, Jimmy, I hope that works," she whispers, touching my filthy sleeve with her clean, soft hand.

"The only other way was for me to go off with my tail between my legs," I says.

"Are you sure you're not pestering the animals without reason?" she says.

"I'm running blind," I says. I take out the picture of the guy who was in Atlantic City with Helen Brickhouse. "This is all I got."

"Danny Tartaglia," she says.

"You know this man?"

"Danny Tartaglia is DiBella's son-in-law."

23

Who doesn't know the joke about the guy who says to the girl, "Would you do it for twenty bucks?" and she says, "How dare you? What kind of a girl do you think I am?" and he says, "Would you do it for a million?" and she goes, "Well . . ." and he says, "Now we know what kind of girl you are, all we got to do is establish a price"?

Everybody laughs at that one, because they think it's true, because street savvy says that everybody wears a tag. Everybody can be bought. There's enough truth in it to make you cynical. Sometimes it looks like everybody in the world is on the take. I suppose the average person, you and me, if we was starving or if our kids was going without shoes or medicine, would sell whatever it is we call honor for a quarter. It's only a step or two before you roll over for a million, or a thousand, or twenty bucks, for a new car or a house or a seat in the front row.

When we roll over, we say we're only human. But we want everybody else to be a saint. We want somebody else to be Jesus Christ and hang on the cross for us so at least we can convince ourselves that there's goodness in us somewhere.

I'm not thinking this when Ray Carrigan, the Democratic party chairman, sends for me. I'm thinking how I'm going to turn him down and still come out with my job and my skin.

After he shakes my hand, he says, "Sit down, Jim. We don't get to talk very much, but I know your

father since we was young men together and I know
you since you was a little kid with your finger up
your nose."

I'm supposed to laugh at that, so I laugh at that.
There are customs like bowing to the queen of England and kissing the Pope's ring which you do even
if you're not a great believer.

"Sit down, Jim," he says, "and pick out a cigar."

I don't smoke, but I take a cigar because it's polite
and because I will give it to my old man.

"Just because we don't have a chance to talk very
much," he says, "it don't mean I don't keep my eye
on the son of Mike Flannery. I ask your leader,
Delvin, what sort you are, and he tells me you're the
best precinct captain he's got, who can even get Republicans to vote the straight Democratic ticket because you're so sweet-natured and good to one and
all."

"Ah," I says, because I don't know how to shovel it
as fast as he does and I decide not to try.

"Other ward leaders got a good word for you, too.
Even Vito Velletri, who hasn't many good words to
say about an Irishman, has good words to say about
you. What's all this leading up to, Jimmy?"

I open my mouth and . . .

"Well, you might ask," he says. "It leads up to the
simple fact that the party's got plans for you. It
wants you should run for the state legislature from
your district in the next election." He sits there grinning at me, waiting for me to kiss his foot.

I got to tell you something else about Chicago
politics. A seat in the state legislature or even the
Congress is nothing but stepping-stones to the job of
city alderman. It's also a way of burying a pest out to
Springfield. I think somebody wants me bought, paid
for, and shipped out of town. Someday maybe when
I want to get back in, I could find the door to
Chicago shut in my face.

"We want you should go over to the capital for a few weeks. Look the place over. Meet a few people . . ."

"No, thank you, Mr. Carrigan," I says.

"Find out where the keys and locks is."

If the cigar dropped out of his mouth I wouldn't have been surprised.

"I don't hear you right, do I?" he says.

"I've just found the woman who's going to be my wife," I says.

"Take her with you."

"She works over to Passavant as a nurse and I don't think she'd give that up so easy."

"If she's going to be your wife, she does what she has to do for her husband's career."

"I don't think it works that way anymore, Mr. Carrigan. Women got minds of their own, even when they're wives."

"Not good Irish girls."

"Well, yes, I think Irish girls, but that don't matter anyway because my lady is raised Jewish."

"That could be a mistake."

"She's a Democrat."

"Even so."

Poppsie Hanneman sits across from me in Shelley's Bar and Grill eating a beef dip and drinking a beer like she ain't one of the number-one society party-givers in Chicago.

"Do you still think of me?" she says, looking up through the curly bangs on her forehead like she used to do when she wanted me to love her.

"I thought of you practically every day up until last week," I says.

"Oh? What happened then?"

"I met a woman."

"Not a girl?"

"Oh, she's a girl, too."

"You're not going to tell me you've fallen ill of

love, are you, Jimmy?" she says, teasing me on the square.

"I feel fine," I says.

She considers my face for a minute. "Of course you do. I can see that. What's her name?"

"Mary Ellen."

She puts down the sandwich.

"What's the matter, don't you like the sandwich?" I says.

"I'm afraid it's going to give me heartburn," she says. "What can I do for you?" she says, making like she's as bright as a penny.

"I want you should tell me about this Danny Tartaglia. I could ask elsewhere, but if you can tell me about him, I'd rather get it here."

"What I know is just beauty-parlor gossip. I don't know anything about his place in the syndicate—if he has one—or his power—if he has any—or his future—if he has one of those. I know what I hear about his marriage and about his love life."

"That's what I want to get from you," I says.

"Danny Tartaglia is not Chicago family. I understand that he was brought in from Philadelphia for some business reason about eight years ago. I think he's an attorney, but I wouldn't swear to that."

"It don't matter," I says.

"Doesn't, Jimmy, doesn't," she says almost absent-mindedly, and I remember one of the reasons I let go of her so easy. I don't mind being corrected—I got nothing against improving myself—but it's the way she does it, offhand, like she's telling her lap dog to sit. When she does it like that, I know she thinks small of me and maybe doesn't love me like she said she did.

"You can see how good-looking . . ."

"I think Tartaglia looks like a weasel . . ."

". . . he is from the picture you carry."

". . . but what do I know?"

"So I suppose it came as no surprise when Theresa DiBella, Carmine's only daughter, his baby, his princess . . ."

"His pudding," I says to myself.

". . . the apple of his eye, falls in love with Danny Tartaglia."

"Which is all right by DiBella?"

"It's never all right when a man's daughter falls in love with another man. Don't you know that?"

"Yes. All right."

"He hates it, but he also wants his little girl to be married to a proper man, an Italian, a Catholic, an educated man with a profession that can be useful to DiBella's own business interests. A man who can serve him, but is not a criminal like himself."

"He blesses the marriage?"

"Oh, yes. He gives the biggest wedding you ever saw. Don't you remember?"

"I wasn't invited."

"It was in all the papers. It was on television."

"I don't . . ."

"I remember . . ."

". . . read the papers much. I don't—"

". . . you don't watch television. You're an anachronism, Jimmy," she says, and then she adds, "That means—"

"I know what it means, Poppsie. Give me a break."

"Theresa gets pregnant almost right away. That's good. They have a daughter. Not quite so good, but so far as DiBella's concerned, Tartaglia isn't so much the husband of his daughter anymore, but the father of his grandchild."

"That's the way it is. DiBella don't have to like Tartaglia to want to make it nice for his family. What does he do for Tartaglia?"

"The usual, I suppose. I told you his business is his business. I've heard DiBella threw some legitimate legal stuff Tartaglia's way and set him up with Velletri to handle some insurance claims. It's the bedroom stuff I've heard about."

"Which is what usually breaks these wise guys in half."

"Theresa has another daughter and then a son. The head of the family can now rest assured that his seed will go on. But Tartaglia apparently loses interest. He's seen in the Loop when he should be home by the fire. He pretends that he's entertaining prospects. It's supposed to look like the girls are for the clients' entertainment, not his."

"Who believes that?"

"Not many. He also has a respectable friend he uses as a beard."

"How respectable?"

"Another attorney with political ambitions and connections to Judge Ogilvie of the appellate court."

"Which is Vito Velletri's judge."

"Don't the stew get thick?" Poppsie said, grinning, and for a second there the girl who fought her way up out of the Tenth ward, which is where the steel mills is, doing what a lot of girls do to get a start—doing what Helen Brickhouse did, only doing it better—is sitting at the table with me, and not some society lady who married well.

"So, it's this connection to DiBella which makes this friend of Judge Ogilvie do the favor for Tartaglia and make like it's him who's hustling the girls and Tartaglia's just tagging along?"

"It's also the friend that tells DiBella the truth when he thinks it's time for him to know."

"When is that?"

"When just about everybody already knows it," Poppsie says.

"So he convinces hisself he's not selling Tartaglia out."

"And he tells DiBella that he'll be happy to pass the word to Tartaglia that he should cease and desist

. . . to stop dishonoring DiBella's daughter and grandchildren, and the family DiBella."

"And when DiBella thinks everything's covered
and Tartaglia's been told, Tartaglia just gets better
and sneakier about cheating on Theresa."

"He moves his action to whorehouses, especially in
the Twenty-fifth."

"And how goddamned dumb can a man get to
start messing around all over again, after he's been
warned, in his father-in-law's own ward?"

"Hey"—Poppsie smiles—"that ain't the way it goes.
What the hell does DiBella care if his son-in-law likes
to play with naughty girls? You think he hasn't done
it, too? Wives are for keeping house, cooking spaghetti sauce, and making babies. Whores are for
giving pleasure and doing tricks which a man's wife
shouldn't even know how to do. Maybe DiBella even
likes Tartaglia better, now that the damned fool is
being discreet about where he has his playmates. My
God, Flannery, you is one of . . ."

"Are."

". . . God's innocents. You see what you've done to
me? I'm supposed to be the good influence on you.
Ten minutes with you and I'm talking as though I
never left the Tenth."

"You'll get all your graces and manners back the
minute you cross the avenue," I says. "Who's this
attorney who's Tartaglia's good friend?"

"No," she says.

"All this you tell me you didn't get from sitting
around under the dryer."

"That's why I'm not telling you the name."

I lean forward and put both of my hands over her
hands. I always liked her hands. They're the part
about her which has changed the least since she
climbed up into the tower. They're as big as mine,
but white and soft. Her nails are long, but not too
long, and they're painted pink.

There were nights, when we was together, when she'd paint them red so they looked like they was dipped in blood. She'd paint her mouth just as red and put spots of rouge high up on her cheeks. She'd lay on the eye shadow and mascara and dress fancy in black and red underwear—"Just so I don't forget" —and they was good nights, because she was so real.

"Don't say it," she says.

"Say what?"

"For old times' sake."

"Okay, I won't say it."

"Favor for favor?" she says after a minute, because I don't let her hands go and she knows I'm not giving up.

"You know it."

"If your Mary ever asks you if you ever cared much about another woman, will you lie and say there was only one, and will you think of me?"

"I won't be lying," I says.

"Tartaglia's friend is Walter Streeter."

"And he's a friend of yours."

"He was until I found out he was in love with Theresa Tartaglia," she says.

"Ain't the stew getting thick?" I says, and grin at her.

I start to pull my hands back, but now she's the one who won't let go.

"When are you going to open your eyes, Jimmy?"

"You got to explain that," I says.

"You say you know what an anachronism is?"

"Something that's out of its right time."

"You're an anachronism, Jimmy. The days of big-city machine politics are over."

"That's what they thought when Byrne took over, but she opened her arms and gave the ward leaders the big hug."

"I don't think this mayor is hugging many of the bosses."

"He ain't breaking their canes either."

"But he will. He will. He'll pick them off one by one when it suits him. There's no place for you anymore."

"He'll just put his own men in their chairs and I ain't big enough to be replaced."

"This city can't be run on patronage anymore, Jimmy."

"They may call it something else, but it won't change. It'll always be favor for favor. I'll deliver my precinct on election day like always," I says.

I know I'm sounding stubborn. I know I'm even sounding a little angry, because deep inside I know that Poppsie's probably right. New power brokers are reinventing the game, rewriting the rules, and I won't be a player if nobody gives me a copy. And if she's right, if nobody picks me, where's that going to leave me? I wouldn't know how to live without doing favors. It's what I do.

She lets go my hands. "Jimmy, take care," she says. "You say you're not big enough to be replaced. Well, maybe you're not big enough to be missed."

24

"What's the nature of your problem, Mr. Flannery?" Walter Streeter says.

He's about thirty-five and long-faced with curly dark hair coming to a widow's peak. His mouth and cheeks look like he expects to be eighteen for the rest of his life, but he's got the fleshy nose of an older man and his eyes are about one hundred and three years old.

We're sitting at the famous old grill over on State Street which is used as a second office by half the lawyers and judges in the city. The lunches are very expensive, but I'm even ready to spring for that so I can have him where he's comfortable. When you're going to ask somebody for something they won't want to give you, it's smarter to get them comfortable.

"You ever try the kidneys and sausages in this place?" I says. "There's nothing like them."

"Mr. Flannery, I agreed to meet you without having my clerk do a preliminary interview because you came recommended by your reputation as a precinct captain in the Twenty-seventh ward."

"And who knows but maybe someday I'll be a ward boss when you want to be a superior court judge, am I right?"

"No, you're not right. I try to conduct my business a case at a time and my life a day at a time. I like where I am when I'm there. I don't spend a great deal of time speculating about the future."

"But you spend *some* time? You got to spend some

time thinking about where you're going to be ten years down the road—twenty years down the road."

"One has an inventory of prudent expectations."

"I couldn't of said that better if I thought about it for a year," I says admiringly. "You know a girl named Helen Brickhouse?"

"Is she part of your difficulty?"

"No. It's more like she's part of your difficulty."

He don't even twitch.

Benny, the waiter, comes over in his rusty tuxedo and stands there with his pad in his hand like he'll stand there for a century waiting for us to tell him what we want.

"You say that you recommend the kidneys and sausages?"

"The best."

"A minute steak, medium rare. Thick-cut potatoes. Peas, but only if they're fresh . . ."

"Everything we got is fresh," Benny says.

". . . French-roast coffee, half and half, not cream."

"I'll have the same," I says.

"Benny lies, you know," Streeter says. "Sometimes the peas are frozen."

"How about Helen Brickhouse?"

"I don't know a Helen Brickhouse."

"How about Helen Addison?"

"I don't know a Helen Addison."

"How about Helen Caplet?"

This time he ain't so good at the game. His old eyes give him away. "Are these all the same girl?" he says.

I take a picture of Helen Brickhouse out of my pocket and put it on the table in front of him. "Same girl, different names. Professional names."

"Is she an actress?"

"She was a whore."

"Was?"

"She's dead."

"If you're involved in a homicide or a willful death, I'm not the lawyer for you, Mr. Flannery."

"You might not be the lawyer I need. You might not be the friend I'd like to have. But you're the man I want to talk to."

His head snaps around and he's looking for the waiter while his right hand is fishing a fat fountain pen out of his pocket.

"Benny," he says, "bring me the check right away." Then he turns to me. "I'm not going to eat the lunch we ordered. I'm going to pay the check because I'm not going to eat it and I don't want you to be able to say you incurred any expense on my behalf while seeking council which I could not give."

"Eat, don't eat. Pay, don't pay," I says. "That's up to you, but I'm telling you that you're going to talk to me. Here or someplace else. Here or maybe one night when you're sitting breaking bread with your friend Judge Ogilvie, who I think maybe does you a small favor by having the case against Joe Asbach put in a drawer . . ."

"Wild speculations . . ."

". . . or maybe when you're kissing up to Velletri or DiBella . . ."

". . . and even wilder accusations are defensible in a court of law . . ."

". . . or maybe when you're with your very good friend Danny Tartaglia and a couple of playmates like Helen Brickhouse."

"I don't know any Helen Brickhouse."

"Ah, you're lying to me, Counselor. Maybe you didn't know Helen called herself Caplet or Addison, but you knew her when she was Helen Brickhouse. You knew her before, or maybe just at the time, she got into the life. You fixed up your very good friend Danny Tartaglia with Helen Brickhouse."

Benny brings the check and the lunches.

"Do you want I should put the plates down or did you decide you don't want to eat?"

"Put the plates down, Benny," I says, "and give me the check. Attorney Streeter's decided to let me treat him to lunch after all."

"Why would I be doing all this?" Streeter says.

"A handle's a handle. You do a special favor for Tartaglia, maybe someday he's in a position to do a special favor for you. That don't work, you always got DiBella, who'll maybe thank you a lot if you talk sense to his horny son-in-law, which ain't got brains enough not to dirty the sandbox. One thing you lawyers learn in law school, that's how to come out ahead no matter who loses, no matter who wins."

"What do you want?"

"I want to know what happened with Tartaglia and Helen."

"How will you use it?"

"To squeeze. Maybe to put him behind bars if I can. To punish him good for what he done, one way or another."

"If this ever goes to trial . . ."

"Then you admit there's a crime?"

". . . I'll deny telling you anything."

"I'm asking you do you think he did murder?"

"What I think and you think has no force in law. I can't place him at the scene of the bombing. Can you?"

"Can you place him at a flat in the Twenty-seventh over to Benjamin Alley?"

"When?"

"Three nights ago."

"I have to think about it. I can't just drag up an itinerary of the week and spell it out."

"It's what you lawyers ask people to do on the witness stand."

"That's the courtroom. This is real life. I'll think

about it. If I remember, it might give him an alibi, you know."

"I'm not out to hang anybody without cause. I got an idea you'll decide about what an alibi for Tartaglia would be worth to you. Tell me about him and Helen."

He starts to tell me about himself and Tartaglia and Theresa. And the story of Helen Brickhouse is in it, too. You got to understand, the way it's being told to me maybe isn't altogether the way it happened, because Streeter's doing his best to make himself look as good as he can.

"I knew Danny in law school. We were not exactly close, but I suppose you could say we were more than acquaintances, perhaps even friends."

Streeter tells me how ambitious Tartaglia is even when they was in school. How hungry for success and money and the best of everything.

"The schools are pouring out lawyers," Streeter says. "We have the most litigious nation in the world, but even before Danny and I graduate, there aren't enough cases to go around because we also have more attorneys per capita than any nation in the world. Incomes are falling. Positions with top firms go to the superstars. You start to think about chasing ambulances."

"I can get lawyers plenty of work, they want work. Poor people who can't find their way through the system, who get their houses stolen away from them because they sign the wrong paper or don't sign the right paper. Old ladies who . . ."

"Certainly. Young lawyers talk about . . ."

". . . get tossed in the gutter because they can't fight the landlords."

". . . doing storefront work. You quickly learn you can't eat good works."

"Or drive it around, or live in it by the lakefront."

"Whatever you say."

I work on the steak while Streeter tells me how both he and Tartaglia decide that the best place to make it after they get out of law school is in politics. Not as candidates, but as advisers, political managers, image-makers, patronage brokers.

"Danny decided to take an even shorter route. He met Theresa DiBella and got her to marry him. Did he love her? Don't ask me. I don't know. He didn't say."

"But you've got an idea."

"Danny loves money and power above everything else. He uses women like food and drink, to keep him charged up. Theresa was a key to the room with the ladder that led to the top. If there'd been an easier way, he wouldn't have bothered with a wife. He should have loved her. I don't see how he couldn't have loved her, but maybe it's just not in him."

He lets his eyes go soft, like he's suffering a secret pain, and I know this Streeter as good as I'll ever know anybody. He's an actor and a liar. He'd tell a lie to an elephant in Africa on the long shot that the elephant is shipped to a zoo in Chicago and tells the story to a talking giraffe which tells it to somebody who might come to Streeter with a deal.

"You met Theresa DiBella the same time that Tartaglia met her?"

"I didn't meet Theresa until I appeared as best man at their wedding."

He makes it sound like it was love at first sight for him, but that he swallows his envy and plays the good friend through the years. Patiently waiting, faithful and true, until maybe Theresa needs him.

"When did Tartaglia start to play?"

"He'd have started before the last note of the wedding march faded away if he hadn't known he couldn't get away with it. DiBella was watching him like a hawk in the beginning, waiting for any sign that this sonofabitching vandal from the East Coast wasn't doing exactly right by his little girl. So, at first, Danny played it very straight. Why not? He was playing for very high stakes and Theresa wasn't hard to take, even as a steady diet, until he got her pregnant."

"Then he started looking around?" I says.

"That's what he wanted to do, but the first child was a girl and didn't take the old man's attention the way a grandson would've done. The next was a girl, as well, but I think Danny was already playing around on the sly by then, and the hell with the chances of being found out. I suppose he thought if a man's careful enough . . ."

"When did he start getting less careful?"

"After the third child was born. It was a boy. As far as DiBella was concerned, his son-in-law had done his duty by his daughter. The old man's little girl and princess was a mother now. Three times a mother. And the mother of the next generation that would carry on because DiBella had no sons to have sons."

"Now he doesn't watch Tartaglia so close," I says.

"That's correct. These old men are realists. They respect the mother and protect the wife. But what a man does outside the home, he does because he has the juices running in him. Because he has big balls like a bull. Because it's what men do."

"So, now Tartaglia starts coming home late and going off on long business weekends," I says.

"That's right."

"And sometimes you go along?"

"That's also right." He calls for Benny. "Benny," he says, "this steak is cold. Bring me another."

"You'll pay for it," Benny says. "You waited too long to complain."

Streeter nods and waves him away.

"Tell me the good parts," I says. "You introduce Tartaglia to Helen?"

"Yes."

"Where'd you know her from? Cicero?"

"I met her the first time in New York."

"You was a customer?"

He shrugs.

"I met her again in Chicago through my interest in art. She was at a showing with a detritus assembler . . ."

"Is that what they call a junk artist now?"

". . . by the name of Bo Addison, a black man of considerable verve."

"Who piles up old tires and bedsprings and who's got a brother that sells women."

"Who has a brother who runs a social club in the Twenty-fifth," Streeter says.

"You're a member?" I says.

"Addison provided privacy and discretion for a price. That's where Danny saw Helen at first."

"Why not use her own flat?"

"She shared with two other working girls. Danny didn't want that."

"You'd think he'd like the chance for special fun and games."

"He didn't treat Helen that way. He treated her like a girlfriend. He almost courted her. Maybe it was just another tricky notion. Acting. You know, like some men have girls dress up like schoolgirls or nurses."

I wonder if Streeter is describing one of his own preferences.

"Anyway, that's how he treated Helen. And she fell for it."

"The whore bought the act?"

"That's how it seemed. She made herself available to him even though it meant cutting down on business."

"What about the loss of revenue?"

"Danny made up for that, I think."

"And anything else?"

"You mean did he set her up in a flat? I don't think he'd gone that far, but I can't swear to it. Danny stopped giving me a play-by-play description of the games they played. That was different for him, too. It might have been on his mind, though."

"He was buying into the routine, too?" I says.

"It looked that way to me. But then she told him she'd stopped taking precautions one weekend when they went to Atlantic City like newlyweds. She told him she'd gotten pregnant that weekend."

"How did he take it? Did he say?"

"He started confiding in me again. It shocked him out of whatever fairy tale they'd cooked up together. She was a whore and he was one of the up-and-coming young men with a wife, three children, and a powerful father-in-law. She was a whore playing the 'game' on him. Trying to screw a big payoff out of him. Maybe ready to do blackmail."

"He was asking you for advice?"

"Oh, no, he knew what to do. He told her to get it taken care of. He told her to take care of it or he'd have it taken care of."

"How do you know that?"

"Because I was there when he told her."

"Did his father-in-law know anything about this?"

Streeter shrugs and shows the palms of his hands up and empty.

"Did Theresa know?"

"She wouldn't have believed it, even if Danny told her himself."

He makes this Theresa sound like a clay pot. I don't think she's a clay pot. She was raised like a Sicilian princess. I figure she's a woman with hot blood. I think she puts up with what she's got to put up with when Tartaglia starts to stray. She puts up the good front as long as he don't make her lose honor. I think maybe she cools off her blood with a white fish like this Streeter. And I think, maybe, when it came right down to it, she could've taken a pesky whore out like she was nothing but a fly.

25

Jackie Boyle sends the list of badge-holders over to my flat by messenger. There's only ninety badges with a two in the middle if it's a three-digit number, but there's one hell of a lot more if it's a four-digit number. It don't matter. There's only sixty-eight permutations either way which have been handed out in the Twenty-fifth. And only one of them belongs to Daniel Tartaglia.

"We're going to Atlantic City," I says to Mary.

"It's almost winter," she says.

"I ain't going to go swimming."

"It isn't gambling, is it? I hope you're not a gambler, James."

"I want to talk to some desk clerks."

"Atlantic City is full of hotels. Therefore, it's also full of desk clerks."

"Just the desk clerks at the Beau Rivage."

"Can't you call?"

"I got to bribe them. You can't bribe a person with a marker."

Mary arranges to take three days off from the hospital with a friend who'll cover her shift for her.

On the plane, she shoves in under my arm.

"You want this should be a honeymoon?" I says.

"Are you so sure of us, James?" she asks.

"I'm sure."

She hesitates, and then she looks up into my face

like she wonders about my ability to protect myself out in the cruel world. She also looks sad. "I'm not so sure, James," she says, "but there's no reason in the world why this can't be just *like* a honeymoon."

Atlantic City is not for October unless you like to watch wheels go around and around taking money out of your pocket.

We check in at the Beau Rivage. The desk clerk is wearing a maroon jacket and a hairpiece. He hands the key to the bellhop, who takes our bags and heads for the elevators.

I ask Mary to go to the shop and buy me some shaving cream, which I forgot to bring along.

"Let me ask you a question," I says to the clerk.

"A question," he says.

"How many desk clerks you got working here?"

"Three shifts, two to a shift, and the man who fills in on days off. Plus the manager and two assistant managers who take a shift now and then."

"Ten. You hire more in summer?"

"Three more."

"How many of the ten people working here now was here last summer?"

"I was here last summer. How important is it that you should know who else was here?"

I put a ten, a twenty, and a fifty down on the counter all in a row. I cover the twenty and fifty with the folded newspaper I got in my coat pocket.

"Maybe it ain't important at all," I says. "Maybe having a look at the June register does me just as much good."

"That would mean four fat files. Have you got the time?"

"The first week maybe will do me."

"Divorce case?" he says.

"Missing person," I says.

He picks up the ten, folds it, and puts it into his pocket. He goes into the office and comes back in three minutes with the boxes of registration cards for the first and second weeks of June, which is to show me he's a thinker.

I flip through the cards top to bottom like I'm dealing a deck of cards. How do I know what name Tartaglia used? I don't, but I figure people don't make it hard for themselves to remember a false name. Even so, I know I got to get lucky because maybe Tartaglia uses the name of some favorite old aunt when he's out cheating on his wife.

But he don't. There it is. He uses the name which Helen goes by in her professional life. Mr. and Mrs. Daniel Caplet, it says.

"You got a copier in the office?" I says.

"We have."

"Will you make me a copy?"

"It's against the rules."

I take the newspaper off the twenty. He picks it up and folds it and puts it with my ten. He takes the registration card and is back again with a copy in no more than a minute. He knows the fifty is still under the newspaper. He don't know how to get it, so he thinks about it while he puts the cards back in the box.

I show him the photograph of Helen.

"I wish I could say yes," he says. "Look around."

Even a glance shows me there's a half a dozen women in the lobby who could pass for Helen Brickhouse if you was to go by the picture of her taken when she's laying dead.

I show him the picture of Helen in the summer dress.

"Still no cigar," he says.

I show him the picture of Tartaglia. He picks it up and studies it for a minute.

Mary comes back with my shaving cream and stands next to me. She knows exactly what's going on.

"I think so, but not if I got to swear," the clerk says.

"Why do you think so?"

"You don't see the type very often these days."

"What type?"

"You know, Rudolph Valentino. I'm a movie buff. I pass the time seeing which guests look like what old-time movie actors."

"Who does he look like?" Mary says, smiling at the clerk and pointing at me.

He smiles back. "Jimmy Cagney," he says.

Mary laughs like she just won a prize.

"Would you be willing to sign a paper saying this man was here at this hotel in June this year?"

"I'll sign a paper that says I *think* he's the man who was here in June this year, or one who looks very much *like* a man who was here in June this year."

"Send a typewriter to my room. I'll have the paper ready for you to sign when we come down for dinner," I says.

"This is not a deposition? This is not an affidavit to be used in a court of law? Is that our understanding?"

"Everybody's a lawyer," I says. I pick up the newspaper, leaving the fifty behind, and take Mary's arm.

"Will a paper obtained in exchange for money stand up?" Mary asks as we walk over to the elevators.

"I don't want it should stand up. All I want it to do is give certain parties reason to consider what they done."

Mary wins two hundred bucks at roulette. I lose ninety at craps. She teases me about it, but except for the ha-ha about who won what, she makes the time in Atlantic City exactly what I suppose everybody wants a honeymoon to be.

26

Back in Chicago, I scramble to catch up on my inspections and my reports.

Also I go around getting signatures on a testimonial saying what a great guy and courageous fireman Mooshie Warnowski was. Also Mrs. Cuva wants I should get her boy on the summer-job program, which there is not even going to be a list for until next March. But there's a list which gets compiled every year *before* the official list, and everybody knows it. So all the mothers and fathers who know somebody have been putting their bids in for their kids earlier and earlier. I figure in ten years the new summer job list will start piling up names the day after the summer program ends.

Also Mary wants to buy some decent furniture for the living room and bedroom. Since this sounds to me like she's making a nest, I willingly go along with it, though there are few things I hate more than walking around furniture stores.

I find time to go down to see Addison, the pimp, one more time.

Jessie opens the door and says, "You got the hots for me, Flannery, I can tell. You keep coming here just to see me."

"It's true," I says.

"Well, you can't have me because you're a milk-faced Irishman who sunburns easy and you all look alike to me."

"Look at it this way, Jessie, you marry me, you ain't marrying a man but a whole goddamned race."

"You're tempting me," she says.

"While you're thinking over my proposition," I says, "can I see the man?"

"Addison is not around. He's down to the art museum with his brother. Believe it or not they're going to give him a room in which he can pile his junk."

"Has it got bars on the doors and windows?"

"It's a special show for six artists who got nobody but theyselves to thank for the fine and original work which they do."

"What will Bo Addison's contribution be?"

"He's going to arrange piles of dog turds preserved in plastic."

"You tell him," I says, "that he stole that idea from the woman who bronzed her baby's dirty diapers and hung them on the wall of a museum over to New York."

"That goddamn town always wants to be first," Jessie says. "So, good-bye. I'll tell the boss you was here."

"Show me to the parlor."

"You don't mean it," Jessie says, showing me two silver dollars with raisins in the middle for eyes. "Are you going to be a customer?"

"And break your loving heart? Oh, no. Just show me the parlor. I'm buying new furniture for my flat and I want to see how it's decorated."

Jessie shows me into the main room. "So you don't want I should send in the lineup?" she says.

"Oh, please do," I says. "I like company while I'm picking out cushions."

Seven girls—all sizes, all shapes, all ages—come into the parlor through the beaded curtain in the doorway.

Ciccone's wife is one of them. She's wearing feathered mules and a red teddy. She looks like a chicken which got plucked.

"What are you doing here?" I says. "Has your husband sent you out to work?"

"I left him. What the hell do I need living in a steam bath?"

"You know a John by the name of Tartaglia?"

She shakes her head.

"You know a John by the name of Streeter?"

She shakes her head.

"I know a John by that name," Mavis Concord says. She's wearing a bra and panties and a fur jacket what is open in front.

"You're Mavis Concord," I says.

"That's right," she says.

"You're my girl," I says.

Gino's ex and the rest of the girls file out of the room.

"How come you know this Streeter's name?" I says. "Does he tell you?"

"Oh, no. He calls himself Smith."

"How do you know it ain't Smith? With so many Smiths in the world, somebody's got to be named Smith."

"When we go out to dinner, he pays with a credit card."

"And you read it?"

"I watch when he signs the receipt."

"He's not very smart."

"He's a lawyer. He thinks he's very smart, and that's not very smart."

"But you *know* you're very smart?"

"Smart enough to know I'm not going to stand here shooting the breeze with you on my time."

"Let's go," I says.

She crooks her finger and says, "Follow me."

I trail her down the corridor to her bedroom, which is behind one of many doors. The room isn't a sleeping bedroom but a working bedroom. She lives elsewhere. It's just large enough for the bed and a chair and a little dressing table. There's two mirrors, one on each wall, so I see myself repeated in them a thousand times into a distance that makes me a little dizzy.

"That bother you?" she says.

"I ain't in love with my kisser," I says.

"Me either. The last trick liked to watch hisself making like an army."

She pulls a string and curtains cover one wall, which makes it a little better. I can only see us once.

She takes off the jacket and starts with the clip in front of her brassiere.

I put twenty bucks on the dressing table.

"Don't bother," I says. "Stay warm."

"Are you kidding?" she says, jerking her chin at the twenty. "That's sixties' prices."

"I've been out of circulation," I says.

"Tch-tch," she makes with her tongue when I add another double sawbuck.

I add another and she stops making like a chicken.

"So, what do you want if you don't want me?"

"When you went out on the town with this Streeter, did you go out alone?"

She smiles like she's way ahead of me and says, "No, we go out with Rudolph Valentino and Helen—"

"That's not his name."

"Of course not. It's who he looks like. I don't even remember what last name he gives us, but we all call him Philly."

"Like Phillip?"

"Like Philidelphia, I think. It's where Streeter and him first got to know each other."

"You don't see his signature on the credit receipt?"

"He never picks up a tab."

I show her the picture.

"Sure, that's Philly."

"Tell me about Helen and Philly."

"That'll be fifty bucks. Your time's up."

"I've only been here five minutes."

"You're buying quality, not quantity."

"I'm buying a whore's time—you should excuse me for not talking nice—which I don't have to buy, if you want to look at it one way. You look at it another, I'm talking to Helen's friend . . ."

"We weren't special friends, Helen and . . ."

". . . or at least her working associate. What happened to her could happen to you someday. Maybe not the same thing in the same way for the same reason, but it could happen you end up on a slab with nobody to care how you got there. Wouldn't you want somebody to care how you got there?"

She's quiet a minute, her eyes going soft and afraid while she thinks about the many bad ways whores come to the end of the line.

"Okay," she says, her voice husky all of a sudden.

"Tell me about Helen and Philly. Was she playing a game on him?"

"More like the other way around. He conned her good."

"His wife didn't understand him."

"His wife understood him too good and he wanted a divorce. But there was kids and it had to be done right, he says."

"He tells Helen he loves her?"

"That's what he says."

"He tells her he wants to marry her?"

"That, too."

"Helen told you this?"

"She also tells me she's going to give him a test."

"She'll tell him she's pregnant."

"She'll do better than that. She'll *get* pregnant and go kill the rabbit with the doctor of his choice."

"So she does it. And she tells him. And he sends

her to a doctor for the test and it comes positive. And he drops the act."

Mavis nods her head every time I come to the end of a sentence.

"And what else does he do?" I says.

"He tells her she's on her own."

"But Helen's not rolling over for that."

"She tells him he better pay up for the abortion."

"But he tells her to go to the free clinic like she's probably done a lot of times before."

"People think women like us go get scraped out like we go to get our teeth cleaned," Mavis said, suddenly angry.

I thought about that for a minute.

"They had one hell of a fight," she says.

"How do you know?"

"The night she told him, Helen comes to my place with a black eye and a cracked tooth."

"Why'd he hit her?"

"She said she'd go to the wife. That's when he hit her, and said she'd better just get taken care of and not try to hold him up, or he'd do a lot more than crack her tooth."

"How did Helen know his real name?"

Mavis shrugs her shoulders and the strap of her bra falls down her arm. "Who knows? He got his pants off most of the time he's around her, ain't he? Where's he keep his wallet? I don't know how she finds out. She finds out."

"I'm going to get what you told me typed out, and when I come back I want you to sign it."

"Don't bother," she says, and gets a portable type-writer and some paper out of the top drawer of the dressing table. "I was a secretary before I became a private businesswoman." She sits down on the chair and rolls three sheets of paper with carbons into the machine. "I can type direct from dictation. Go ahead."

"Put the date at the top," I says.

Her fingers rattle on the keys.

"To whom it may concern . . ."

"Hey," Mavis says, "you know stenography's fifteen dollars an hour and typing's five dollars a page with two carbons?"

"That's only for professionals," I says.

When we're done, she signs it and I fold it up and put it in my pocket.

"This Joe Asbach a customer of yours?" I says.

"Sure."

"The day Helen was killed in the explosion over to the clinic on Sperry was you with Asbach?"

"Sure. I was with him when he went over in a cab to see was his people walking in circles."

"He go inside?"

"No, he had his hand up my skirt and other things on his mind."

27

It's not hard to find out where Daniel Tartaglia lives. It's a big house with a fence and gates on the North Shore not very far from where his father-in-law, DiBella, has his estate. I park my coupe on the other side of the street from his driveway, in the shadows of a big shade tree, ready to wait as long as it takes for him to come home.

After half an hour, I see somebody in a jumpsuit come down the drive and through a little door in the main gate. It's a hard-looking man about fifty years old who walks up to my window and raps his knuckles on it. I roll the window down.

"You come in the house," he says with a heavy accent.

I don't bother making a case for innocence. I look up over the tall hedges on the other side of the fence and tops of the trees between the hedge and the house and I see the window in the tower room where somebody is standing.

I follow the man through the door in the gate and up the drive. As we approach the house, I see *three* Dobermans mock-fighting with one another. We're twenty yards away when my escort peels off.

"You go on up to the door," he says, and walks down a side path toward the garden at the side.

His voice alerts the dogs. They stop fooling with one another and look at me. I stand there with my knees locked and they stand there stiff-legged, too. Then they start stalking me, going down low to the ground, their necks stretched and heads out, watching every move which I ain't even making.

"Jesus, Mary, and Joseph," I says to myself. There's times when, even if you don't believe, you believe.

A little girl about seven comes whipping around the corner wearing a little red shirt and blue overalls.

"Get back," she says, stepping right in front of those animals, and whacks each one of them a shot in the chops. They laugh at her, forget me, and start kissing her hands and trying to kiss her face.

"It's okay," she says. "Who do you want to see?"

The front door opens up and a very attractive woman with dark hair and olive skin set off by a dark-red jumper and white blouse is standing there, looking at me.

"Mr. Flannery, is it?" she says.

I touch the brim of my hat, feeling like one of my old Irish ancestors doing honor to the lady of the manor.

"Come in. Don't mind the dogs. Angelina's made it all right." She steps aside as I walk past her into a hall with a ceiling three stories above the tiles. I smell a perfume like old roses.

She shows me into a sitting room, as big as my whole flat, off the hall on the left side of the main stairway. It's so quiet, it's like being in a convent. The air's warm and the light sunny, like it's always summer in the room because this woman wants it that way.

She's not exactly beautiful, maybe not even pretty. Words like that don't even apply.

"You shouldn't lurk," she says, and smiles at me.

"I wasn't lurking. I was waiting for Daniel Tartaglia. Am I talking to his wife?"

"You're speaking to Mrs. Tartaglia," she says, making the difference that she wants to make for reasons of her own. "Please, sit down."

The chair, made of pale wood and covered in

some kind of shiny fabric with little flowers on it, looks like it'll break, but I see the one she sits in, which is just like it, holds her weight, so I take a chance.

She leans forward a little in her chair. "I'm not going to offer you a drink or . . ."

"I don't drink."

". . . a cup of tea . . ."

"I don't want nothing."

". . . because you're neither an invited nor a welcome guest in my house. You're a witness."

"This is a nice room you got here, Mrs. Tartaglia," I says. "This is a very beautiful home you got. The grounds is big enough to make a park, where maybe fifty kids could play, down in my precinct. You look like a nice woman and I got no reason to want to hurt your feelings . . ."

"Did I hurt yours?" she says, her eyes widening as though she's surprised that a dog should complain about such a thing.

". . . even though what you say to me sounds like an insult. I just want to make it plain to you that I come from a good family, just like you believe you come from a good family, but my family ain't bandits and they ain't thieves. What we got, we didn't squeeze out of somebody's else's veins or grind out of somebody else's bones."

"You take chances. You take incredible chances," the soft voice of Carmine DiBella says from the doorway.

I didn't even hear the door open. I didn't hear his footstep on the rug. He's standing there in slacks what cost more than the clothes in my closet, wearing a silk shirt and cashmere sweater and four-hundred-dollar hand-made loafers. He looks like a million bucks and is worth maybe twenty times that, but he's a water rat what comes from water rats that made the millions beating up and killing people that

couldn't fight back. He knows that, and he knows
what I think of him.

"You dare to scold my daughter," he says.

Faced with somebody like me, DiBella's kind got
two things they can do: blow me away or act like I
ain't worth a bullet or a sharp blade. Since I got him
in a glass box with what I done over to Poppsie's
dinner party, he has to manufacture a lot of con-
tempt for me. Make me something he can wipe off
his shoe.

I can go on with it. I can tell him that he made his
daughter what she is: an insolent, spoiled woman
who turns to her father to smooth every bump, sop
up every puddle, sweep every leaf off the road. I can
go jump under a truck, too, if I'm dumb enough.
There's a point beyond which I can't push, or DiBella
will have me done and worry about cleaning up the
mess after.

I stand up. "I say what I say with all due respect,
Mr. DiBella. I can't let anybody take my face."

"All right, all right," he says, waving his hand that
I should sit down. I see a gleam of respect in his eye.
He thinks I'm dumb, but also a little brave.

Theresa gets up and lets her father sit down facing me. She stands right in back of him with her
hands on his shoulders, like they're having a family
portrait done.

"You cause me a lot of bother, a lot of worry,"
DiBella says.

"I'm sorry," I says.

"I don't condone what happened to the old woman."

"She was an innocent bystander." There's a little
edge to the way I say it.

DiBella's mouth twitches a little, warning me to be
careful.

"I don't condone the killing of the pregnant girl,
either."

I don't trust myself to reply to that. I just nod my

head the way he nods his head, blessing the truth of the remark.

"The nurse was the worst," he says. "That was very wrong. That was very stupid."

"It was murder, pure and simple," I says.

"It came after."

"After what?"

"After I was asked the favor." He stares at me as though I could be a devil, or maybe I could be the priest who's hearing his last confession. "I hate this," he finally says. "I hate that you put me in a place where I've got to explain myself. I'm not used to having to explain myself."

Theresa's hand moves. Her finger comes up and touches the skin on the side of his neck. He moves his head a little, toward the hand of the person he loves most in the world.

"You're entitled," he says. "Here's the way it comes to me at first. I'm told this Joseph Asbach will be picked up for conspiracy to create a civil disorder and do public damage because a bomb has gone off at the Free Abortion Clinic on Sperry Avenue. My son-in-law, Daniel Tartaglia, appeals to me to use my influence in Asbach's behalf because Asbach is a client, and also because my son-in-law supports the principles of the Right-to-Lifers . . ."

"Even when they blow up . . ."

". . . although he certainly does *not* endorse the use of violence to make their case. Asbach, who's a friend as well as a client, swears to Daniel that he had no hand in the bombing and has not one bit of knowledge about it."

"So you do your son-in-law the favor," I says. "Why not? It's a terrible thing these people are doing, killing unborn babies. It's unfortunate maybe that the bomber wasn't more careful and two people die, but that's the chance people take who go against

God's law. Besides which, it's such a small favor. A telephone call."

"A telephone call," he repeats very softly. "Judge Ogilvie makes the arrangement."

"Then you find out somebody put a bullet in Helen Brickhouse and set the bomb to cover it. He's not a very good assassin, or he don't care, and Mrs. Klutzman dies, too."

He nods. "It's not such a simple favor anymore. I have Joseph Asbach brought in for a conversation. I let him know I'll see he's rearrested if he had anything to do with the killing of the girl, or if he knows anything about the killing of the girl, but that I'll see he has the best defense money can buy. I'll see the charge is reduced to voluntary manslaughter. I'll make it easy for him."

"Which is when he tells you that Daniel Tartaglia was playing house with Helen Brickhouse?"

He nods again. "Which is when—"

"If Danny wanted to wallow with pigs, that was all right with me," Theresa says, "but to pick one out and fool himself that he'd fallen in love with her . . ."

"Hush, Theresa," DiBella says, reaching back to touch her hand with his hand. "Asbach tells me about my son-in-law and his foolish indiscretion. So, now I call my son-in-law in for a conversation."

Theresa gives a little gasp as though we've come to the part that humiliates her most. She lets go her father's shoulders and walks away over to the tall windows. She pushes the sheer curtains aside and looks out at the garden. I can hear her little girl shouting at the dogs.

"Does he admit that he played a game with the whore what went too far. Was she threatening him with blackmail?" I says.

"He says no," DiBella says. "What does it matter? He's the father of my grandchildren. I already asked the favor. I already gave my marker to a lawyer . . ."

"Streeter."

". . . a judge . . ."

"Ogilvie."

". . . and a committeeman."

"Velletri."

"I can't look like a man who changes his mind like he changes his shirt. I can't tell them to take away Asbach's shield."

"Ah, Mr. DiBella, you're blowing smoke in my eyes. You ask me into this house and say you're going to treat me to your confidence. You're going to explain to me, as much as you hate having to do it, how you got caught in a ball of string . . ."

A little storm of noise comes from the hallway and right through the door, which opens and lets in a little girl and a little boy followed by the man who looks like Valentino. The kids run to their grandpop and climb all over his shoes and expensive slacks with their dirty shoes, and he don't even care. Tartaglia loses his smile and stands in the doorway looking from Theresa to DiBella to me. He takes it all in and he knows what's happening.

DiBella is leaning over the two kids what he's set down on the floor off his lap. He's taking pieces of candy from his pocket and pressing them into their little hands, and he's whispering love songs into their little ears.

"Oh, Pa," Theresa says when she sees what he's doing with the candy, like any mother in the world would do when she worries about the kids' teeth and sees Grandpop slipping them candy.

"So, what can a little licorice hurt them," DiBella says over his shoulder. "It's natural licorice," he says to me. Then he shoos the kids out to play with their big sister and the dogs. Tartaglia closes the door behind them.

"You don't have to hear this," DiBella says.

"Yes, I have to hear this," Tartaglia says.

"Your father-in-law's just telling me how you asked him to do a favor for a somebody you said was a friend, but it turns out you was asking the favor for yourself."

"How's that?"

"You was killing the investigation into the Sperry Avenue bombing which would have pointed to you sooner or later."

"You have evidence to back up these allegations?"

"Shut up, you want to stay," DiBella says. "Shut up. This isn't lawyer talk, this is talk between honorable men."

I don't know how I got put in the bag with an honorable man who made his pile with the gun and the knife, but I'm in no mood to argue fine points.

DiBella turns his flat eyes to me again. "Yes," he says, "my daughter's husband used me like you say. He told me a little lie to cover a bigger lie. He asked me to get a little favor done which became a big favor."

"You could've let go."

"No. I couldn't let go. I told you this man is the father of my grandchildren."

"And my husband. Still my husband," Theresa says.

There's a lot of pride at stake here. A lot of face. Tartaglia hears what's in his wife's voice. It sounds to him like it sounds to me. Now that he's scared enough, sorry enough, she'll have him back. He takes the chance and walks over to stand beside her at the window.

He smirks at me because he's really sure of himself when she doesn't move away. DiBella will protect him. He won't get tossed to the dogs.

"You had the autopsy report and the bullet taken from Helen Brickhouse tossed away," I says.

"I had that done," DiBella says.

"You sent Connie and Angie after me."

"You wouldn't back off. It was just to hurt you a little."

"You ever see that goddamn junkyard dog?" I says.

"The watchman was in the shed. He'd have come out and pulled the dog off before you were damaged too much."

"You asked Velletri to talk to my Chinaman," I says.

"You don't listen to your Chinaman. You made Delvin look bad."

"He had to go all the way to the party chairman."

"So you see how it escalated? I did a small favor and it ends up I'm in debt to Ray Carrigan, not to mention Velletri and Delvin." He makes it sound like it's all my fault.

"You corrupted the police a little along the way, too," I says. "You got Pescaro, a good cop, to put three murders in a drawer."

"I didn't get him to do that," DiBella says, splitting the hair, making it clear he *asked* the favor but didn't *execute* the favor.

"Not murders," Tartaglia says, ready to dazzle us with what he knows about the law. "Homicides—"

"Shut up," DiBella says without even turning around.

Theresa takes her husband's hand and gives it a squeeze, telling him to quit while he's ahead.

"The father of my grandchildren is right," DiBella said. "There are no charges in these deaths that concern us. There's no evidence on which charges can be based."

"I found out some things. I can maybe find out more."

DiBella shakes his head slowly. "No, no. Mr. Flannery. Don't you see you got nobody to take it to even if you dig up any gold? Don't you see there are too many people involved now who can't back down? Be smart. Better. Be wise."

I get up. The back of my legs feel like they're about to snap. I know what an old fighter who's lost his last fight feels like. I hate the way Tartaglia's raising his eyebrow at me and the way DiBella's even looking a little sorry for me. I walk across the twenty-thousand-dollar rug like I'm walking out of a boxing arena covered with old cigar butts, shuffling my feet, looking for a place to lick my wounds.

"Mr. Flannery," DiBella calls after me.

I turn at the door.

"You got my marker."

"Mr. DiBella," I says, "I don't want to do business with you."

28

I put all the stuff I collected on the kitchen table. Mary and my old man look at it like it's stuff taken from the tomb of some ancient king.

I put down the picture of Helen Brickhouse I got from Captain Pescaro, which was taken after she's dead at the morgue. I put down the pieces of the snapshots and the enlargement I got from Flo Brickhouse, which was taken on her daughter's holiday visit to Atlantic City. The copy of the register from the hotel in Atlantic City and the deposition I got from the desk clerk goes next to them.

I got a deposition from Bo Addison what identifies Daniel Tartaglia as the man who came to see Helen at his place more than once, and another from Mavis Concord putting the finger on him, the guy what looks like Valentino.

There's the copy of the application for honorary deputy sheriff, which is signed by Daniel Tartaglia. And, finally, there's the badge, once issued to Daniel Tartaglia, which has been delivered to me with a note from Carrigan saying it came to his attention that I had an interest in such a badge with such a number and he wants me to know it's been an inactive badge for more than two years.

"So favors is still being asked, and still being delivered," Mike says.

"It don't never seem to end," I says.

"By this time everybody's scratching up the leaves, covering the messes what they made."

"They're still afraid of you, James," Mary says. "Still worried that you won't let go even now."

"This Tartaglia just about admitted . . ."

"Just about?" my old man says.

". . . that he done it."

"Can you make a case on just-*about* a man confesses? Can you make a case on depositions from a pimp and a whore? An affidavit from a desk clerk in Atlantic City who'd swear to anything for twenty bucks."

"He remembered."

"You want to tell me you didn't give him at least twenty bucks?" my old man says.

I don't say anything.

"And, yeah, a badge number which Mary remembered had a two on it which there are how many such numbers? One of which they are ready to swear has been out of circulation for two years?"

I feel like my mouth is filled with rusty iron. I'm biting the nail.

"There's three people dead," I says. "You can't leave me with just that and six bits for the altar candles."

"That's what they left you with, Jimmy," Mike says, "just a prayer."

29

You'd think nobody cared much about that little whore what was killed. It looks like Helen Brickhouse is not even a memory, except to her mother and father, and maybe to me, after a month goes by.

I find out on the quiet that Daniel Tartaglia is being very good and has maybe even decided to settle down and enjoy family life. Especially since he finds out, like few men ever have the chance to find out, just how much his wife—the wife what he did so wrong by—is willing to forgive him.

But Bo Addison don't forget, because maybe he really cared some about Helen. And his brother the pimp don't forget because he was using her to maybe bring Tartaglia down, which would maybe bring Ogilvie down, which would maybe put the squeeze on Velletri so that the mayor and the party chairman figures it's time for a black alderman, like Addison, in the Twenty-fifth.

And I don't think Walter Streeter forgets because I'm pretty sure, after all's been said and done, that he's the one who keeps me informed about Helen Brickhouse every inch of the way because he wants Tartaglia out and himself in. Into DiBella's good graces. Into the heavy action on insurance cases. And into Theresa's bed.

"You blew the whistle on your good friend once," I says to Streeter.

We're sitting in the restaurant on State Street again,

and Benny's just finished laying down our meals, steak for Streeter and sausages for me.

"When it don't take," I goes on, "you blow the whistle on him again, only you help his misbehavior along a little the second time by tossing Helen Brickhouse at him. You know what he likes. You write the script for her. In a way you're as much responsible for Helen's death and for Mrs. Klutzman's death as Tartaglia is."

He sets his face like he's going to protest.

"Don't explain me the law," I says before he can do so. "I know it and you know it."

"I truly never thought . . ." he says.

I wave the rest of it away. "I'll give it to you. You certainly never thought he'd go after the nurse what saw his face and kill another nurse by mistake. I'll give you that, but for the other, you were in it up to your neck."

"It's all over," he says, not mean or angry, just pointing out the facts of life.

"I want your help," I says.

"Yes?" he says, like he's waiting for his orders.

"You know how it goes," I says. " 'Screw me once, shame on you. Screw me twice, shame on you. Screw me three times, shame on *me*.' "

"You're too far ahead of me."

"I wouldn't want to be the one what screws DiBella the third time," I says.

I see he's getting an inkling.

"You know and I know that your friend Danny ain't going to stay at home and true-blue forever. He's got an appetite and it don't go away. He'll be buying ass again."

"If he does, he'll buy it as far out of town or as deep under the covers as he can get," Streeter says.

"Oh, yes. And he'll need help to make connections. He'll need a middleman. He'll need you."

"Wait a minute . . ."

"He still don't know how you tried to give him the shaft. He still trusts you. He still trusts that pimp, Addison. He'll accept your good services."

He leans forward a little. What he wants and what I want is making us partners, if not pals.

"I know about a girl who just come in from Detroit. She's eighteen, maybe nineteen. She reminds me a little of Helen Brickhouse, but not too much like Helen Brickhouse."

"You in business with her?"

"Oh, no. Neither do I try to save her soul. She already knows what she wants to do. I tell her there's other ways, but she knows what she wants to do. I tell her to come to me if she gets in trouble. She comes to me the other night on a procuring. I see that she walks and I find her a room with Addison."

"Yes?" he says, and now we're conspirators.

"You talk your friend up, you work him up. You tell him he's got to live on hamburger, maybe forever, when all the time there's guys feasting on the biggest hot table in the world out there."

"Is that all I do?"

"You make the introduction. You maybe even loan them your apartment the first time so they should get it on with nobody the wiser. Along the way we move them to a flat, a little place with a hidden mike. A flat where we can take pictures if we have to. And then, one day, I put out the word. It whispers through the town. It gets to the ears of a man like DiBella, who makes it his business to hear everything and . . ."

30

The weatherman promises snow, but it's already spring and there ain't no snow. The day is warm with sun and clear skies.

They've fixed up the little stands on the courthouse steps and wrapped the rails with red, white, and blue bunting for Emmanuel Warnowski Day.

Mrs. Warnowski, wearing a new black dress and a hat with a veil, is sitting up there on the platform with Mooshie's fire captain, the fire chief, the commissioner, Delvin, Ray Carrigan, half a dozen aldermen, a Polish priest . . . and the mayor.

I sit with Mary in the first row of the audience, which is not all that small, filled as it is with off-duty firemen and derelicts from my Twenty-seventh who maybe knew old Mooshie.

The priest says a prayer three times, once in Polish, once in Latin according to the old Mass for the dead, and once in English. I think how much quicker Rose Klutzman was sent to wherever souls are sent than the priest is sending old Warnowski.

After him comes Delvin, who goes on for some time about good public servants.

Next come the commissioner, who reads Mooshie's citation, which praises him for his fine display of courage when, while racing to a five-alarm fire, he deliberately crashes his car, thereby saving the lives of a nun and her class of parochial schoolgirls who is going back to school from an outing at the zoo.

The mayor hands the Widow Warnowski a medal, and there are a few happy tears. And it's over.

I feel a tap on my shoulder. Ray Carrigan, the party chairman, is standing there.

"Hello, Jimmy," he says. "Ain't it terrible what I read in the paper about Daniel Tartaglia?"

"It looks like somebody gave him back his badge," I says.

"It looks that way. Ain't it ironic he should get shot down in a house, in which working girls was allegedly plying their trade, by a pair of thieves?"

"Investigating, no doubt."

"No doubt."

"Ain't it lucky he wasn't in the room with one of them? The poor girl could've got killed as well."

"Well, God rest the poor man's soul."

"Amen," I says.

After Carrigan leaves, the mayor passes in front of me. His aide whispers in his ear. The mayor stops and looks me over. "So, you're Flannery, are you? I've got to hand it to you."

"Sir?"

"Mooshie Warnowski."

"A good man. A hero."

"Flannery," the mayor says, "you really can shovel it high."

The Six-Hundred-Pound Gorilla

Everybody knows the one that goes, "Where's a six-hundred-pound gorilla sit? Anywhere it goddamn wants to sit."

My name's Jimmy Flannery and I ain't a comic. I work in the Sanitation Department of the City of Chicago reading flow meters and inspecting pipes, and I'm a precinct captain for the Democratic party in the Twenty-seventh ward.

I don't know how many of you remember the terrible winter of '78, when corruption and bad organization make it so they can't clear the snow off the streets and gives Jane Byrne the crack into which she hammers a wedge and busts the machine apart.

Well, it nearly happens again this past winter. The cold is so bad the furnaces in many municipal buildings breaks down, among them the one that keeps the zoo warm. Even the polar bears is sneezing.

Baby, the beautiful female gorilla and the star attraction, is the one they're most worried about. Somebody comes to me and asks do I have any ideas where to keep her until the furnace is fixed. I suggest the Paradise Bath House over to Chadwick Avenue, which has got steam rooms, wet and dry, and a heated pool where they can give her a bath if she needs such a thing.

So they take her there and put her in a steam room with just a little humidity in the air, it should feel like the jungle.

The next morning, when her keepers go to give

her breakfast, she's cowering in the corner crying, and there's two naked men, smashed to bloody pulp, sprawled dead on the wooden benches.

Watch for *The Six-Hundred-Pound Gorilla* by Robert Campbell, coming soon from Signet Mystery.

ABOUT THE AUTHOR

Robert Wright Campbell has written extensively for television and the movies, and is the author of several novels published both here and abroad. His screenplay for *The Man of a Thousand Faces* was nominated for an Academy Award. He currently resides in Carmel, California.

The Junkyard Dog is the author's first mystery for Signet books.

⊘ SIGNET MYSTERY

SUPER SLEUTHS

(0451)

☐ **ACCIDENTAL CRIMES by John Hutton.** It was the perfect place for murder... a lonely road through a desolate moorland. And in the killer's twisted mind, they'd been the perfect victims: young and pretty, hitchhiking alone after dark..." A dazzling psychological thriller..." —*Publishers Weekly* (137884—$3.50)†

☐ **NIGHTCAP by J.C.S. Smith.** Someone had taken Lombardo's reputation for drop-dead chic too literally—but to have gotten up to the penthouse without using the locked elevators, the killer would have to be deadlier and far more cunning than the subway rats Jacoby was used to chasing... (137736—$2.95)*

☐ **THE GREAT DIAMOND ROBBERY by John Minahan.** There were twelve diamonds, famous and flawless. And three suspects, all no-name, Class B hoods. There had to be a Mr. or Ms. Big, pulling the tangle of strings that leads Rawlings all the way to England... and a spooky aging beauty with a family secret that makes the Godfather's look tame...
(135717—$3.50)*

☐ **DEADHEADS by Reginald Hill.** Is Aldermann pruning some people as well as his prized roses? His boss, next in line to be "deadheaded," thinks so. And so do Inspectors Dalziel and Pascoe, called in to investigate a chain of grisly coincidences that may turn out to be murder most exquisite—and most fiendishly undetectable... (135598—$3.50)*

*Prices slightly higher in Canada
†Not available in Canada